KU-794-857

"Looks like somebody saved the taxpayers a lot of money, doesn't it?"

Harry Calahan surveyed the limousine that had belonged to the late Carmine "Bubby" Ricca, acquitted only that afternoon on a charge of murder. Someone had evidently not agreed with the verdict. Ricca, his attorney and his bodyguards lay very dead as a bespectacled technician collected evidence.

"Calahan, what are you doing here?" Detective Lieutenant Neil Briggs had arrived, and the sight of Harry had him fuming.

"This is one you're gonna need me on."

"Need you?" Briggs bellowed. "You get your lying ass in gear and get the hell back to that stake-out squad you're on loan to. Everytime you go out on the street, we got somebody screaming police brutality."

Harry looked back coolly. "You're a good man, Briggs," he said. "And a good man knows his limitations—you're gonna need me . . ."

Magnum Force

novelization by MEL VALLEY
based on an original screenplay by
JOHN MILIUS and
MICHAEL CIMINO
from a story by
JOHN MILIUS,
based on a character
created by
HARRY JULIAN FINK
and RITA M. FINK

Star

A STAR BOOK

published by
the Paperback Division of
W. H. ALLEN & Co. Ltd

A Star Book
Published in 1978
by the Paperback Division of
W. H. Allen & Co. Ltd
A Howard and Wyndham Company
44 Hill Street, London W1X 8LB
Reprinted 1978, 1980

Originally published in the United States
by Warner Books, Inc., 1974

Copyright © 1974 by Warner Bros., Inc.

Printed in Great Britain by
Hunt Barnard Printing Ltd., Aylesbury, Bucks.

ISBN 0 352 30238 0

This book is sold subject to the condition that it shall
not, by way of trade or otherwise, be lent,
re-sold, hired out or otherwise circulated without the
publisher's prior consent in any form of
binding or cover other than that in which it is published
and without a similar condition including this
condition being imposed on the subsequent purchaser.

Chapter I

A tangle of reporters and cameramen was gathered in the corridor outside the courtroom. After a wait of several hours they had grown anxious and giddy. They were passing the time exchanging witticisms and cynicisms when suddenly the courtroom doors flew open. The newsmen surged forward, rushing the uniformed policemen and private bodyguards who had been stationed at the doors to hold them back.

First out of the courtroom was a phalanx of a half dozen cops. Following immediately behind was Carmine "Bubby" Ricca, with Nat Weinstein, his attorney, in tow. The instant Ricca's large-featured face became visible in the doorway, an explosion of flashbulbs went off, handheld cameras started to whirr and floodlights turned the hallway brighter than daylight. A dozen bobbing microphones swarmed around him. He accommodated all the commotion by cracking a grin so wide that the lights reflected off his gold-capped molars.

In spite of the abdominal flab showing through his opened jacket, Ricca was fairly hefty and well-built, a middle-aged man with black hair and a swarthy complexion. He looked especially natty in a sharkskin suit and a fire-engine-red tie. Standing erect at taller than six feet, he greatly diminished Weinstein, his short, pale and eager-looking functionary who seemed to be having difficulty adjusting his beady eyes to the television lights.

Ricca advanced a few steps into the corridor and then stopped to take in the chaotic scene. As if listening to all the shouting at once, he focused on a single reporter who had almost dropped his microphone while jostling a cop to gain a few inches. It amused Ricca to have the uniforms on his side for a change. He had once remarked face-

5

tiously to a colleague that the police could best serve the city by helping little old ladies cross puddles while delegating the responsibility for enforcing law and order to others far more qualified, such as himself.

"Mr. Ricca! How do you feel about the acquittal?"

Ricca's eyes brushed over a reporter's extended microphone and held his grin. Then he pushed on as bodyguards closed in around him on all sides. His silence, compounded by a pair of diabolical eyes, caused the press corps to grow even more restless, and scuffling broke out in the crowd.

"Mr. Ricca! Mr. Ricca! What's your feeling on the court's decision?" This came from one reporter in the surging and persistent throng whose voice fell deeper, and therefore sounded louder, than the others.

"Any comment, Mr. Ricca?"

"Will you sue for false arrest?"

"Mr. Ricca, is it your opinion that the D.A. is harassing you?"

The questions came as rapidly as the spit-fire shots of a Thompson gun, a pace to which the notorious mobster could no doubt relate. But he continued to maintain his silence—and his grin—as he treaded down the corridor, lips sealed. Finally the attorney, Weinstein, shouted over the chorus of questions, attempting a statement.

"I don't know why they waste the taxpayers' money," he said, his voice nearly screeching on this civic-minded note. He paused, locking his face in the hard scowl typical of Mafia lawyers, and added, "This whole thing was an arbitrary attack on a legitimate businessman. How much longer will the public allow this sort of thing to go on?"

Ricca nodded to indicate that he liked the attorney's way of putting it. Just as he did so, a press camera crashed to the floor and a cameraman fell, backwards, clutching his groin. The cameraman was trampled underfoot in the subsequent confusion. Not until several moments later, and about ten feet further down the corridor, did another reporter, braving the police and Ricca's private army of bodyguards, bull in to within inches of Ricca to try again, haltingly and through sputtered breath, "Do you have any comment, sir?"

"Wha?" Ricca demanded.

"Have you any comment on the court's decision, Mr. Ricca?"

"Comment?" Ricca pondered brusquely, as if trying to unlock the meaning of the word. "Yeh—their minds are dead!"

Amused with himself, Ricca laughed and extended an arm around Weinstein's shoulder, a signal which Weinstein obeyed by laughing too. Grinning himself for the first time, but talking through it, the attorney offered a bit of elucidation on his client's earthy comment.

"I think what Mr. Ricca means is that he's happy with the decision," was the way Weinstein paraphrased it.

Behind the two men, the next figure to come out through the door was a man who walked alone. He did not appear to be quite so jubilant. To the contrary, he seemed immensely disenchanted. His name was James Estabrook, the chief prosecuting attorney on the Ricca case, a man with a Yale law degree and a strained sense of righteousness. His expression contained that look of exasperation common to hampered government prosecutors. These moments were always painful to Estabrook because he was obligated by breeding—as well as by direct order from the D.A.—to contain public displays of anger to a level no more flagrant than his gray suit. The cameras, leaving Ricca momentarily, turned on him, and the glare of the lights showed him to be a very drawn and very tired man indeed.

"Any comment, Mr. Estabrook?"

Estabrook found a camera to pour his eyes into.

"Mr. Estabrook, sir, how do you feel about the court's decision?"

He feigned contemplation for a moment, musing that inevitably there seemed only two answers to this question. After all, one was usually either elated or despondent on such occasions, and this time Estabrook found himself, as was so often the case lately, to be the latter. He nodded slightly, cuing the camera, and then limbered his lips to

7

invite silence. His adroit reply was a practiced brevity that said more than an hour's harangue.

"This is not the first time this has happened," was the succinct phrasing he used. For a moment he considered leaving it there, but then decided to complete the thought: "And it will probably happen again."

His gaze into the camera remained unblinking as he then gathered his lips and decided against any further comment, no matter how tempting.

"I have nothing more to say at this time," he said. He activated his elbows and carved himself an exit through the crowd.

Outside in front of the Hall of Justice, on this brisk, sunny San Francisco afternoon, the sidewalks had been barricaded by police in their attempt to hold off a hundred, perhaps two hundred, angry demonstrators who composed the dissident faction in Ricca's labor union. When Ricca and Weinstein appeared on the steps, they let out a roar of unadulterated enmity. Several placards denouncing Ricca in crude and bitter terms bobbed in their midst, the most notable being one with the word "KILLER" angrily lettered in dripping red paint on a white background.

But if the demonstrators had any effect on the union leader, he failed to show it. Ricca's face held the steady grin. He even enlarged it for a moment when, in the manner of General Eisenhower, he flashed the crowd a two-finger victory salute. The irony that this very same gesture was also offered, in some quarters, as a peace symbol amused him. Dropping his arm, he continued down the steps to the sidewalk where, at the curb, a limousine was waiting. He stepped into it as if nobody were watching.

Through the window Ricca's grin could be seen turning smug as the limousine started to pull away. This infuriated the demonstrators, a knot of whom overran the barricades to hurl fists and obscenities at the retreating car. A reporter singled out the demonstrator who had the distinction of putting the last solid kick into the mobster's fender and asked, "Sir, what do you think of the court's decision?"

8

"You want to know what I think?" growled the man, shirttails out, eyebrows arched, his arms flailing. "I'll tell you what I think! Fuck the courts! They waste too much time worrying about the rights of killers on the street! That's what I think!"

Since having been transferred to the night shift, Charlie McCoy had fallen into a habit of sleeping late into the afternoon, sparing just enough time after breakfast to catch a few minutes of the Six O'clock News before leaving for work. On this especially bright late May afternoon, the shades on the windows of his Nob Hill studio apartment were drawn against the lowering orange sun. At one darkened wall was a console television, playing loudly. Charlie had just finished his coffee when a reporter gave the lead story of the evening from the sidewalk in front of the Hall of Justice.

"Shortly after three o'clock this afternoon," the reporter began, "the Appellate Court here in San Francisco acquitted Carmine 'Bubby' Ricca, the union leader and alleged racketeer, on charges of complicity in the murder of labor reformer Anthony Scarza and his family last year in Daly City. The jury delivered the verdict after only ten minutes of deliberation. Ricca's attorney called the trial 'an arbitrary attack on a legitimate businessman' and 'a waste of the taxpayers' money.' Outside the courtroom, police battled dissident labor demonstrators who protested the court's decision. The demonstrators—followers of the late Scarza—surged through the barricades when Ricca stepped into a waiting limousine. Prosecutor James Estabrook called the verdict . . ."

The sound cut off as Charlie McCoy switched off the knob. The television screen dissolved to a flickering point of light and then diminished into total grayness. McCoy paused briefly at the console, taking note of a framed photograph of himself hanging on the wall just above it. The photo portrayed him as a rugged outdoorsy-looking

9

man dressed in a police uniform. Charlie still saw himself as having much the same sturdy aura, though in fact it had long ago dissipated. The photo had been taken seven years before and the intervening time had added fat to his brawn. Also, his face, once so young and vibrant, had wrinkled considerably. His once clear aqua-colored eyes had gone through an especially sad aging process. In the photograph they stood out lucid and penetrating, but in Charlie, seven years later, they had begun to turn foggy and nervous, if not a bit crazed.

His gaze shifted from the photograph to a wall covered with a series of medals and trophies he had won over the years for his excellent marksmanship. Even though he was considered an expert with a heavy handgun, viewed by many as second only to Harry Calahan on the entire force, McCoy was not, or so it was rendered in some official quarters, that good a cop. For this reason he had been consigned for all his years of service to Traffic, left there to contend with the violations of aberrant drivers rather than with the real criminals, like Carmine Ricca, whom he despised. Looking at these awards, certainly his proudest achievements in life, it pained McCoy no end to think that for the remainder of his career he would probably never be anything more than a traffic cop, albeit one recognized for his skills on the target range. Then again, he rationalized, perhaps all that mattered anymore anyway was knowing how to use a gun, and knowing how to use it well. Over the years he had become increasingly distressed by the law's inadequacy in protecting society from the ravages of criminals. He even believed the time had come for police to answer to a higher dictate than law to rid society of certain destructive elements.

On a table beside the television lay his police service revolver, half in and half out of a holster. Next to it was the same SFPD motorcycle helmet he had first donned ten years before. Grabbing the gun and the helmet with one swoop of the hand, Charlie McCoy headed for the door and what he privately promised himself would not be just another night of writing traffic tickets.

Chapter 2

The limousine carrying Carmine "Bubby" Ricca raced southward along Highway 101, leaving behind the San Francisco skyline with its pastel buildings reflecting the orange hue of the setting sun. Three hours had passed since his acquittal, and Ricca, wasting no time, was headed to the airport for a flight to Los Angeles, where he intended to persuade, by whatever means necessary, a few hard-core Scarza followers in the L.A. chapter that they would remain much healthier if they gave up their delusions and rejoined the rank and file of the union. Since he never traveled anywhere alone, he had Weinstein with him, in the back seat, and Tony, his personal bodyguard, was up front next to the driver. The four men rode in silence until the driver, whose name was Tony also (so the right one would know to jump when Ricca said so, he had taken to calling the driver "Also"), routinely checked the rear-view mirror, where he found a most unwelcome tail practically hanging on the bumper.

"Cop!" he exclaimed.

Ricca turned around quickly. When he saw a motorcycle with an ominously flashing red light, he muttered an elaborate obscenity under his breath. If he had told Also once, he had told him a hundred times, "Don't speed." It was not so much that Ricca believed in obeying the traffic laws—which, ironically, he did—as it was that every time he got a ticket the police inevitably used it as an excuse to draw out a whole legal production. Not lingering for more than a brief glance, he turned around again to a normal sitting position and then, leaning forward, took the heel of his hand and slapped the driver on the back of the head.

"I'm driving this thing like a baby carriage, Carmine,"

11

Tony Also protested in a voice bordering on pleading. "Honest!"

Ricca, knowing better, snickered threateningly.

The driver shook his head in frustration and slowed the car onto the shoulder. The motorcycle pulled up behind. A car whizzed by in the right lane. Traffic on the highway was unusually light.

The officer's boots resounded on the pavement as he approached the Ricca limousine. The sun, at that moment, was in its final descent under the wrinkled velvet-like verdant hills, and the glare all but obscured the man's face. The driver stared him down menacingly. Unperturbed, the officer gestured with a pinkie for the man to roll down the window.

Also pushed a button and the window came down electronically. For a salutation, he spit contemptuously, his wad barely missing the officer's recently shined boots.

The officer did not so much as wince.

"May I see your driver's license please, sir," he said.

The driver blinked at the word "sir," probably because it was the first time anybody had ever addressed him that way. Feeling a newfound strength in having been grandly promoted, playing for Ricca, Tony Also demanded, "Do you know who that is sitting back there?"

The words came out sharply and he underlined them with a fierce over-the-shoulder nod.

"I still have to see your driver's license, sir," the officer maintained in the same calm voice.

"Well then, I guess I'll have to look and see if I can find it," was Tony Also's snide reply. Slowly and deliberately, he began frisking his pockets, sighing uninterestedly with a face that made it perfectly clear that he knew precisely where he kept the license.

"Do you know why you're being stopped?" The officer seemed to suggest by the matter-of-factness of his tone that he would have put the same question to Governor Reagan, were he driving the car.

The attorney leaned forward from the back seat. "Yes, officer, we know why we're being stopped—and you're making a big mistake," he said, scowling. The threat was evident equally in his words and his expression.

But the officer chose not to recognize it, explaining patiently, "You crossed over a double line back there."

"Is that so?" Weinstein sneered. "Whatever you say." The attorney shifted uncomfortably in his seat, as if to contain his less reasonable urges. In the front seat, the bodyguard's eyes flickered. Ricca snarled. But through all these menacing indications, the officer remained almost totally expressionless. It became evident to the men that the cop might be just simple enough to uphold the law in the face of all their taunts.

· The driver resigned himself to reaching into a final pocket, where he pretended to discover the license.

"Oh, here it is," he said, passing it through the window. "I just happened to find it."

The officer took it and walked back to the motorcycle, where he checked it against a clipboard full of numbers which the driver mistook for a hot sheet.

"That's right, Simple Simon," Tony Also stuck his head through the window and called back tauntingly. "Go ahead now and check to see if it's stolen."

Once again the officer, appearing very much a man of iron will, considering his consistently unwavering reaction to all these abuses, pretended not to hear. Rather, he went about writing out a ticket. Ricca, piqued by the officer's attitude, told Weinstein, from the corner of his mouth, "I want this bastard busted right out of his job."

"I'll get on it as soon as we get back, Carmine." From Weinstein's eager nod, it was apparent that he would relish the assignment. A strong sense of vindictiveness was one of the attorney's myriad unreasonable urges.

When the officer brought the ticket to the window, he glanced into the back seat, eye-drilling Ricca. Then he turned to the driver and asked, "Is this car registered to you?"

For the first time his tone of voice seemed a shade different—a little higher, a little colder—and the suggestion it seemed to leave was that he really didn't care to

13

know the answer to his question. Or perhaps he already did. Nonetheless, the driver responded. Tony Also, throwing a thumb over his shoulder to indicate Ricca, said, "To him."

"I'll have to see the registration, .please," the officer continued.

"First gimme my license back," the driver demanded, continuing to do all he could to make the ordeal as trying as he possibly could for the officer. Since he knew Ricca would blame him for the ticket whether or not he were really responsible. for it, Tony Also hoped his arrogance might dissuade the officer. But ultimately he needn't have wasted the energy.

The officer, moving to hand back the license, drew a long-barreled .357 Magnum—an awesome gun—from his holster. Without a moment's hesitation he raised it and began firing into the car. The driver got the first two bullets square between the eyes. A hand, still clutching the license, twitched, and then his shattered head slumped down, blood running into his lap.

Ricca and Weinstein froze, dumbfounded by this unanticipated turn of events. For one crucial instant they were too shaken to react. By the time they went for their guns, it was too late. The officer jammed his .357 into the window and shot a number of incredibly quick blasts. Ricca was hit first, then Weinstein, then the bodyguard. The already silenced shots were further muffled in the leather interior of the car.

All of this took less than ten seconds, if even that long. When it was obvious that Ricca and his associates were dead, the officer withdrew his gun, calmly returning it to the holster. A car passed on the freeway, but the driver, apparently having seen the motorcycle and uniform, had eyes fixed on his speedometer and failed. to see the four men slumped over in the limousine.

After shooting one last look into the car, smiling when he noticed the driver still holding the license in his dead hand, the officer returned to the idling motorcycle, mounting it as casually as he might had he just finished writing a boring speeding ticket. He pulled back on the freeway and rode off into the final rays of dusk. A plane came in low over him, preparing to land at San Francisco International Airport.

Chapter 3

Inspector Harry Calahan was a man of many oddities, not the least of which was the manner in which he ate—rather, devoured—his meals. As much as he enjoyed it, Harry regarded the act of eating as an inconvenience, and therefore often tended to it at the same time he took care of other matters. It would not have been an altogether unusual sight, for instance, to see Harry blasting his Magnum at the heels of a fleeing criminal with one hand, while snacking on a hot dog from the other. Sit-down eating was simply not one of Harry Calahan's pleasures in life. Rather, he was the ultimate eat-and-run artist. He could do both at the same time.

Even when time allowed a meal in a restaurant, such as it did one slow spring evening when he and his partner were cruising the Fillmore district on their way back from an uneventful stakeout, Harry still preferred the take-out snack. One of his favorite take-out haunts was a small diner called Joe's, on Fillmore Street, where he stopped before heading back to the police station to punch out for the night.

A sharp wind whipped up a small maelstrom of dust and litter on Fillmore Street as Harry hurried through the doorway of the decaying diner. Though Joe's was not very appetizing to look at—the facade was a patchwork of half-peeled green paint on white stucco and the neon sign spelling "Diner" flickered in its last throes of electrical life, with the "n" and the "r" already deadened—Harry enjoyed the hamburgers and tried to make it a practice to pick up one whenever he drove by.

When he emerged from the diner he had a brown paper bag soiled with grease stains in one hand and a paper container of coffee in the other. At the curb, he scanned

16

up and down the street and then crossed through the first opening in traffic. On the other side was an unmarked police car, where his latest partner, Inspector Early Smith, waited for him behind the wheel.

Smith was a pleasant-looking middle-aged black detective with a Genghis Khan mustache which formed a roof over his frequently smiling mouth. In one respect he resembled a handsome, sprightly, good-natured pirate, yet in another he could easily be mistaken for a white civil servant with black skin. As Harry got into the car with his lunch, Early Smith fired the ignition and pulled out into Fillmore Street, the main drag of the Fillmore district, an area infamous for winos, junkies, rats, poverty and crime. A pastel Harlem West.

With eyes riveted on the street, Harry peeled the waxed paper from the hamburger and immediately began to wolf it down ravenously—without so much as even looking at it. To Harry, food was something to eat, not taste, a style that did not go down well with his new partner.

Early Smith was a more formal man, in spite of an upbringing as the son of a Georgia sharecropper. As Harry gobbled away, Early couldn't help shooting him a sidelong look of disapproval. It was not a vicious or recriminatory glance; it was one of amused censure. In fact, so as not to be misunderstood, he underlined it with a playful grunt. All of this, however, proved a bit unappetizing to Harry, who paused abruptly in mid-bite to chase Early's eyes off his mouth.

"What's the matter with you?" Harry demanded, showing irritation.

"You eat like that all the time?" Early joshed.

"More often than not," Harry replied coldly and finished the bite. "Why? What's it to you?"

"Well—you *shoot* good, but you sure as hell *eat* like shit."

Harry shrugged, shifted his eyes back to the street, put his mouth back to the bun and finished off the hamburger in three enormous bites. Then he wadded up the waxed paper and paper bag, pitching them over the seat onto the back floor. Early, who had taken all this in from the corner of his eye, frowned and pulled the car over to the curb. He jammed into park, leaning over the seat to retrieve the litter, which he then deposited in a plastic container dangling from a knob on the dashboard.

"Is this why they call you 'Dirty Harry'?" he inquired tolerantly, pulling the gearshift back down into drive.

Harry's face tightened at the question. He was on the verge of delivering some assuredly understated caustic reply, as was his way, when suddenly his eyes connected to a flash in front of the car. Blinking, he saw a lanky young black dude, all legs and cool, stalking across the street clutching what appeared to be a dozen new shirts. Three other black dudes followed closely behind him.

"Slow down," Harry called to them from the window. This had the opposite effect, causing the foursome to run faster. Harry squirmed and started for the door.

"Hold it." Early put an arm to Harry's elbow. "These are brothers. Let me handle this."

Harry shrugged. "Okay."

Early rushed out the door and dashed around the car to the curb. The black dudes, however, smelling cop, broke into a sprint. Harry watched from the car, uncapping the coffee container, a thin smile inching over his lips.

"Police officer!" Early shouted. "Hold it!" This prompted the dude with the shirts to zoom into a full run.

"I said hold it, brother," Early called, a tone of no nonsense. It was not altogether apparent that he was using the word "brother" to indicate an affinity with his own race. It sounded more like he meant it to mean "Bud" or "Mac."

The dude stopped sharply, disgustedly kicking a foot into the pavement. Early approached, walking fast. He flashed a badge. As he did so the three other black dudes caught up with the one who had the shirts and they all crowded in closely, their arms extremely restless with canes and umbrellas. Early caught his breath, and gulped. The four flashed disparaging looks at him.

18

Refusing them the satisfaction of seeing his anxiety, Early turned to the dude with the shirts and addressed him with equanimity, asking: "Do you have a receipt for those?"

The answer came in a chorus of hostile laughter.

"Answer me," Early insisted.

The dude with the shirt, grinning broadly and playing to his friends, panned, "Damn! I just threw it away. How do you like that? Isn't it a shame? I don't keep receipts, you know. Not enough room in the pockets. Do you keep your receipts, Tom?"

"Yeh, Tom, how about it?" a second dude snickered, and then the other two joined in also.

Early looked evenly at the one with the shirts.

"What do I look like to you?" he tried reasoning. "Some kind of new man or something? Now, this is no joke, so would you fellas please be good enough to let me know where those shirts come from?"

By all taking a few uncomfortable steps in Early's direction they indicated that no, they would not be good enough.

"Now look here, brothers," Early, an extremely patient man, advised, "let's be smart."

"Don't *brother* us, you Uncle Tom motherfucker," the dude with the shirts sneered derisively. His words were charged with venom.

"Yeh—you black honkie," the second dude jeered, spitting at the ground near Early's shoe.

Meanwhile, Harry, having noted this entire sequence from the car, opened the door and stepped out.

"Hold it a second," he ordered, walking up.

The reply was four sets of eyes bulging in contempt at Harry's humorless white face.

"Come here," Harry, chewing gum, nodded at the dude with the shirts. Coming from his throat, the words showed an enormous control that he immediately belied when he seized the dude by the arm.

"Fuck off, pig," the dude scowled.

"Now, now, just a minute," Harry said, again from his throat. "I want to ask you something in private." He

19

extended his arm around the dude's shoulder in mock friendliness and pushed him into an alley a few feet away.

The dude tried to slip out from under the hold. "Get your hands off me, pig," he protested, but not until they were in the alley did Harry finally remove his hand from the dude's shoulder. And even then, he did so only to seize him by the throat instead. The dude gagged. Harry's grip on his neck was so unyielding that for a moment it looked like the dude would vomit. Without knowing it, he crushed the shirts against his chest.

Harry eased the grip slightly and said, "Look, you little punk. If I ever hear you call a police officer 'pig' again, I'll squeeze your fucking eyes out." In spite of the violence in the words, he did not raise his voice. Yet he meant what he said—literally—and to be sure the dude fully comprehended this fact, he added, "You understand me, asshole?"

Fear and hate in his dark eyes, the dude nodded affirmatively. Satisfied, Harry shoved him out of the alley and back to the others, where he found Early still intellectualizing on the laws of property.

Harry interrupted his partner's discourse by injecting, "Now, George here tells me that the shirts come from Greenblatt's Clothing, around the block. Isn't that right, George?"

The dude stiffened and would not reply. Harry moved, obviously planning to apply other means of persuasion, but the mere threat of what those means might have been proved persuasive enough.

"That's right," the dude blurted out.

Harry signaled for him to hand over the shirts. The dude obeyed.

Early was stunned.

"Now get lost, all of you," Harry ordered. Even before he completed the sentence the four dudes were off and running.

"Aren't we going to take them in?" Early, stunned even further, wanted to know.

"Hell no," Harry told him. "We're not on Homicide. Remember? Besides, it's not worth all the paperwork and a day of my time in court for them to be thrown back on the streets again tomorrow."

Early's eyes gulped as he digested this. He was strictly a by-the-book man and it unsettled him to see the law so compromised. Yet he knew well enough that it would get him nowhere to argue the point.

"What did you do to that kid, anyway?" he asked Harry, starting back to the car.

"I told him that I was president of the NAACP," Harry replied, smirking. He retrieved his coffee from the roof of the car, opened the door and threw the shirts into the back seat. Just as he was getting in a voice crackled excitedly on the radio.

"Twenty-one to headquarters! Twenty-one to headquarters! I just found four DOAs up here on 101, the last exit before the airport, heading south . . .".

"Jesus," Early said.

"Four!" Harry marveled. "Come on. Last exit. Let's pass by and see what it's all about."

"That's not for us," Early protested, extremely disturbed by the suggestion. "You know that."

"Look, Smith, if you don't like it, go work for the post office. I didn't ask for you and you don't have to stay with me if you don't have the stomach for it." As usual, Harry spared no words.

Early clutched the wheel tightly, shaking his head. He gathered his face and started to say something, but whatever he intended to say, he added humor and changed it at the last moment to: "I always make it a rule to take care of my stomach. Good care, as a matter of fact."

Harry simply looked at him with a what-kind-of-stupid-answer-is-that expression.

Early, unfazed by this harassment, continued. "No matter where I am, I treat my stomach like a king," he said. "As a matter of fact, back home in Georgia we used to drop a line right out the door. Those fish never saw ice. One minute they were swimming around in the water, and the next thing they knew my old lady had them swimming around in butter."

Harry, draining the last of his coffee from the cup, came close to smiling at this amateur diversion.

"You ever do any fishing?" Early asked him.

"No."

"Man, you kidding?"

"No."

"Well, if you haven't tried fishing, you don't know about living." Early began to laugh.

"Maybe so," Harry conceded, a thin edge of scorn back in his voice, "but I *can* tell you a thing or two about dying. Now, take this thing to the last exit south before the airport. Quick!"

Chapter 4

A virtual fleet of police vehicles—cars, trucks, mobile labs—surrounded the Ricca limousine in an area cordoned off from the freeway and flooded by searchlights. An unmarked sedan carrying Inspectors Early Smith and Harry Calahan wheeled off the highway and into a security checkpoint. The cop who manned the checkpoint recognized the men and waved them through.

"This your case, Harry?" he called.

Harry only waved back, preferring not to hear the question. As Early found a place to park, Harry took in the scene, focusing primarily on the numerous white-smocked lab technicians scouring the area and the car for clues and evidence. All four doors and the trunk of the limousine were open, with a series of lights attached to the inside. After parking, Harry came up from behind the limousine and poked his head in. Early hung back uneasily.

"Hello, Walter," Harry greeted a technician working, inch by inch, around the bodies in the car. The seats were stained with blood. It was quite a gruesome sight.

The technician, adjusting his glasses, turned around. "Harry?" he said, somewhat shocked. "What are you doing here?" Implicit in the man's tone of voice was a suspicion that Harry wasn't supposed to be there.

Harry ignored the question, fixing his eyes on the lifeless Ricca.

"Well, well," he sighed, "looks like these jokers finally got lunched up real good. Couldn't have happened to a nicer bunch of people."

Walter, jolted and embarrassed by the frankness of this remark, resumed work. Just as he did so a deep gravelly

23

voice commented, "Looks like somebody saved the tax-payers a lot of money, doesn't it?"

Harry turned, his eyes confirming the worst. The voice belonged to Detective Lieutenant Neil Briggs. Briggs was a dark-haired career officer in his late forties, a very intense, antagonistic and humorless man.

"Calahan! What are you doing here?" he demanded sharply. "You're on loan to stakeout."

It was not a question, but an accusation. Briggs was greatly annoyed by the sight of Harry. There was much hostility between the two men, many years in the brewing, and to the extent that they'd suppressed it for so long—or perhaps attempted to tread lightly around it—their relationship had grown into an altogether unpleasant affair for both of them. Briggs had been Harry Calahan's supervisor since the late sixties and had become increasingly frustrated and infuriated with Harry's style, a style that, Harry maintained, required no supervision. Harry had a habit of taking orders as mere suggestions, nothing more.

"I had nothing hot today," he replied coolly. "And besides, I was close by."

"Close by!" Briggs shouted, now completely undone. "Calahan, get your lying ass in gear and get the hell back to the stakeout squad!"

In spite of the volume in Briggs's voice, Harry remained unmoved. He turned to the limousine for another look. "Who do you think did it, Briggs?"

"Look, Calahan. Let's get something straight. You're not a detective tonight. You're on loan to stakeout. Now get out of here!" This time Briggs shouted even more loudly, and his rasping voice caused a number of heads to turn.

"Mm," Harry said, eyes still in the car.

"Calahan, damnit, I said you're on stakeout!"

"Yeh, I know. You saw to that," Harry played evenly.

"I got nothing personal against you, Calahan," Briggs replied stiffly. "But we can't have the public crying 'police brutality' every time you go out on the street."

"I'm afraid you're going to need me on this one, Briggs.

24

I've seen a lot of guys shot. The joker who did this job was very good. Maybe even almost as good as me, from the look of things."

"You really are a killer, Harry. So if this is a good job, you'd sure be the one to know. I don't in the least doubt that."

"A killer?" The word caused Harry to wheel around and meet Briggs square in the eyes. "I just work for the city, Briggs."

Briggs began breathing heavily, turning red-faced. He was furious. "So do I work for the city, Calahan. And longer than you. And it might interest you to know, in light of your record, that in all the time I've worn this badge I never had to take my gun out of the holster once! Unlike . . ."

"You're a good man, Briggs," Harry offered. "A good man always knows his limitations."

Briggs stiffened further, rippling with rage. He eye-bolted Harry and then turned abruptly on his heels to stalk off, fuming. He took two steps and knocked straight into Early, who'd been standing innocuously on the side-lines. Briggs looked him over accusingly, and without a word huffed past. Early, shaking his head, sighed relief and moved up to Harry. He had no further words, either. Calahan frustrated them all.

"What's that, Walter?" Harry wondered, watching the lab technician climb out of the car with several plastic trays full of potential evidence. A small card with a hole burned through the middle had caught Harry's attention.

"It's a driver's license," Walter told him. "With a bullet hole through it."

"Let me see it." Harry examined it closely.

"It doesn't look at all like the usual gangster crap, does it?" Walter speculated, and then, in a confidential aside, added, "Briggs has his nose up his ass tonight, Harry."

"Maybe that's where he thinks his promotion is," Harry remarked, still looking at the license.

"Yeh," Walter laughed, retrieving the license. "Later, you guys." He left.

Harry stood back from the limousine and gave it one

last curious look. Early, watching him, wanted to know. "What's between you and Briggs, anyway?"

"Jealous," Harry uttered, barely moving his lips. "This is the kind of job I should be in on and he knows it. They all know it. It's just a question of time till they call me in."

"Whew," Early said. They headed back to the car. As they walked, Early spotted a group of uniformed policemen shooting glances at him and changing money. One of them had an especially sinister grin on his face.

Harry saw it and laughed through his nose.

"What the hell is that action?" Early demanded uncomfortably.

"They're giving odds on how long you'll stay alive working with me," was his matter-of-fact reply. As Harry stepped around the car, Early hesitated at his door, growing greatly disquieted.

"You're kidding?" he asked hopefully as he opened the car door and got in. Harry fired the ignition.

"I'm used to it now," Harry replied, shrugging. "In fact, maybe I should put down a little side bet myself. I could use the money."

His eyes suddenly wide as saucers, Early asked, not really wanting to know, "You have a regular quota or something?"

"More or less."

As he said this, Harry pulled the car into gear and drove back onto the freeway. He moved to the far left lane, speeding along the miles of fence that bordered the airport. A Boeing 747 came in low, not more than a couple of hundred feet above the car. Approaching the exit, he moved back suddenly to the right and veered off, following the "Departure" signs to the terminal building. Early remained silent and thoughtful for a few minutes until he finally coincided his thoughts with words, asking, "How long did your last partner last?"

"Two weeks." Harry's tone was more appropriate for reciting the score of a ball game.

"God damn!"

"He's luckier than most, though. He's still alive," Harry grinned. "He's a college teacher. You have another trade, Smith?"

"No!" Early seemed offended by the question.

"Too bad."

"Do you?"

"No, but Bill MacKenzie does." Harry spoke softly, as much for himself as for Early.

"Bill MacKenzie?" Early did not recognize the name.

"He's a retired homicide detective."

"What's he do now?"

"You'll see," Harry said. "Are you hungry?"

"Hungry?" Early was incredulous. "How the hell can you be hungry after seeing what you just saw?"

"Seeing what?" Harry asked.

Early found himself with neither word nor gesture to respond to that. They parked the car and took an escalator up into the terminal building, where Harry turned in to a snack stand.

"This is what Bill MacKenzie does," he said. Just as he did, MacKenzie, a portly man with a florid face, glanced up from behind the cash register, where he stood counting out a customer's change.

"Harry!" MacKenzie livened. "Have you heard the news? It was just on the radio. Our old boy Ricca finally got it. Maybe there's hope for the world yet."

"Yeh," Harry answered, unenthused.

"Whad'll it be today?" MacKenzie asked, raising his eyebrows. "Usual?"

Harry nodded. MacKenzie prepared and handed him a taco. Harry, as usual, immediately began to wolf it down.

"How about you, fella?" MacKenzie turned to Early. "Chili and garlic bread are the specials today."

"Nothing please. Thank you," Early begged off, holding his stomach.

"In broad daylight and at close range, huh? Musta looked like some ripe melons," MacKenzie continued as he wiped the counter, but Harry was no longer listening to him. Rather, he was taking in an earful of several

27

frantically hushed voices emanating from the corridor. He put down the half-eaten taco, wiped his mouth on his sleeve and moved out in the direction of the voices, eyes narrowing. Early, still queasy, started after him, a puzzled look on his face.

MacKenzie was saying, "Yeh, I can remember the Floyd case. Got it with an axe during the rush hour . . ." when he finally realized that he was talking only to himself. "Hey—how about some cream pie?" he called. But Harry was already out of earshot, heading down the corridor to a scene taking place near an airline boarding gate. A knot of people in airline uniforms was gathered around two expensively dressed men in their late fifties or early sixties. Everybody was trying to talk at once. As Harry approached he caught these snippets:

". . . there seem to be two . . ."

". . . all in twenties, a quarter of a million . . ."

". . . won't release anybody . . ."

". . . shoved through and were on board before . . ."

"Wait a minute! Enough!" one of the two men in business suits cut in. "Don't all talk at once. Let's get this organized. We can't do anything unless we're organized."

The second executive began the process of organization by turning to a security guard to ask: "Now, Phil, you first. How did they get by you?"

But before the man had a chance to answer, Harry barged in with a question: "You people have some kind of problem here?"

One of the executives flushed with irritation. "I'm sorry, sir," he said sternly to Harry, "but will you please excuse us. It's nothing we can't take care of ourselves, thank you. Now, if you've got any other questions, please take them to the information counter in the main lobby."

Harry replied by flashing his badge. "I'm a police officer."

"You are?" The executive turned eagerly interested. "Thank God! We've got two hijackers aboard our Detroit flight. They want $250,000—we've got that here—and an overseas pilot, who's on his way. We're waiting for the F.B.I. . . ."

"They want an overseas pilot, do they?" Harry said, a glint in his eye.

Chapter 5

Early Smith's jaw dropped as he looked on in near horror, watching his partner, newly decked out in a dark blue uniform and a cap with a gold-braided brim, pace confidently through the boarding area to the loading ramp. Harry took the ramp two steps at a time until he reached the top, where he pounded on the cabin door with his one free hand. In the other hand he clutched a suitcase. After a moment the door cracked open a bit, where it remained for a brief spell before swinging fully open. Harry entered swiftly. The door, operated by an invisible hand from the inside, slammed quickly behind him.

Once inside, Harry found himself greeted by the barrel of a small-caliber pistol. He concentrated on the gun and then looked up into the tense face of the man holding it. The hijacker, breathing heavily, signaled for Harry to hand over the suitcase. But when Harry proved too slow in responding, the man grabbed it himself. The gun still poised stiffly in one hand, he eagerly unlatched the case with the other and, in the manner of a man driving and reading a map simultaneously, gave it a quick inspection. He found it stuffed with what seemed to be an uncountable number of twenty-dollar bills.

"Shall we count it?" Harry quipped. He spoke only with his lower jaw. The upper jaw remained virtually unmoved, and this seemed to contribute a tension to the words, which were not otherwise underscored by their low-volume delivery.

"You just fly this mother, man. NOW!" The hijacker, a tall and wiry man of indeterminate nationality, gestured toward the cockpit with the gun. To emphasize the urgency of this demand, he began shoving Harry down the aisle, causing him to trip by row after row of terrified passengers glued to their seats. Three frightened stewardesses were huddled in the small kitchen area at the head of the first-class cabin. Upon seeing the strange face in the familiar uniform, their faces grew even more anxious. One brought a hand to her mouth in terror, which the hijacker failed to see. Harry leveled her with his eyes.

The hijacker shoved Harry into the cockpit, latched the door behind him and headed back into the cabin. In the cockpit, Harry was confronted by a second hijacker, a swarthy and stubby little man with shadows for eyes. Harry figured him for an Arab. The man wielded a large automatic and used it to direct Harry into the captain's seat.

"All right," he growled. "Get this thing up—and no funny stuff."

Harry took the seat as if it had always belonged to him. From the casual manner in which he conducted himself, it was difficult to believe that the impending flight was not to be just another routine afternoon's work for him. He chewed gum and glanced over the instrument panel, pretending to find it no less familiar than the dashboard of an automobile.

The uniform made him appear even more convincing as a pilot. It fit his tall, lean and dapper frame very well, with the hat accentuating his high forehead and strong, sensible-looking, clean-shaven face. His movements were swift and confident. Only the copilot blinked, but he too could almost believe that Harry indeed was a pilot—that is, until Captain Calahan reached for the headphones and proceeded to clamp them on backwards. This made the copilot, a young man in his early thirties, flinch, but before correcting Harry's mistake he caught himself and bit into his lower lip. But he continued to stare at Harry, hoping for some gesture that might indicate what was going on. Harry offered him no clue.

Twisting his neck around until his chin was over his shoulder, Harry asked the hijacker, "Where to?"

"Just get this thing UP!" the hijacker screamed, growing jittery. He jammed the automatic into the back of Harry's neck and added, "Then I'll tell you where."

Harry's reply was almost cheerful. "You heard the man," he told the copilot. "Let's get rolling here."

The copilot closed his eyes for what seemed to be an abbreviated prayer. Then, reluctantly, he began the instrument check, reading a series of technical names from a clipboard. Harry responded to each affirmatively and with complete authority. When the list was exhausted the copilot, after a short hesitation, signaled the ground crew.

Within moments the boarding ramp was pulled away, and the engines were started, growing from a whine to a roar. With hands on various levers, the copilot began backing the plane out slowly. Meanwhile, Harry, behind the wheel, was all concentration, fiddling with various logs and charts. His eyebrows were furrowed. The copilot again attempted to engage his eyes, but his gaze was intercepted by the hijacker. He turned away quickly.

Hands starting to vibrate nervously, the copilot continued backing the plane out of the terminal area. Harry's eyes rose a degree above the charts—though this was not apparent to the hijacker—as he watched with unadulterated attention, mastering the way the copilot used the throttle, brakes and other gear.

Meanwhile, the sight of the plane starting to move on the ground caused Early Smith, who'd been waiting nervously at the gate, to turn white. An assessment of his features gave every indication that he was on the verge of fainting. Though he'd been well aware of Harry Calahan's reputation before the orders had come through making him Dirty Harry's new partner, he would have never believed—or, for that matter, never even have imagined —that *any* police officer would go to these lengths, would do something so incredibly bold as try to foil a hijacking by taking the wheel of a Boeing 727, when no matter how things turned out, it was as likely that he would be busted for insubordination as it was that he would be commended for his valor. For a brief flash Early couldn't help admiring Harry, but the admiration was quickly washed away by visions of how Briggs would most assuredly react to this latest Calahan play. Early watched the plane, seeing the passengers' faces pressed to the windows.

Inside the cabin, the passengers sat rigid in fear, in what the airlines call the upright position. The first hijacker, buoyed because things had finally gotten under way, took up a position at the tail end of the aisle and amused himself by leveling a pistol at the temple of a stewardess who was doggedly trying to render comfort and reassurance to a terrified female passenger.

Meanwhile, wheeling the plane onto the runway, all systems go for a takeoff, the copilot, overwhelmed by his anxieties, began to lose self-control. He turned to Harry, and in the process of doing so caught the engineer's eyes and used them to bolster his own. When Harry felt the eyes all over him he turned, smiled admonishingly, then nodded and took over the controls.

"Move it!" the hijacker demanded, flexing the automatic.

"Right," Harry replied. He revved up the motors and the plane inched forward. But then, as he reached for another lever, the copilot went to stop him, shouting something at the top of his voice over the roar of the engines. Harry, unable to hear him, eased up on the throttle. Again the copilot shouted. This time he came across loud and clear: "EXCUSE ME, CAPTAIN, PARDON MY ASKING, AND THIS MAY SOUND SILLY, BUT CAN YOU FLY THIS THING?"

Harry's reply was cheerful and to the point. "No."

The copilot's eyes flared. The engineer turned so white he almost disappeared. The hijacker froze for one stunned moment, which was in actuality no more than a mere second or two but was just enough time to allow Harry to simultaneously stand on the brakes and pull back the throttle, which had the effect of hurtling the man against the instrument panel. Harry jumped up quickly as the hijacker's finger twitched on the automatic. He reached inside the captain's jacket and drew a .44 Magnum, doing so almost faster than the eye could comprehend, and used it to club the hijacker senseless. The man, unsuccessful in

3

getting off so much as a single shot, dropped to the floor.

Harry spun around and raced back into the passenger section, where the sudden stop had created near pandemonium. People were screaming and trampling over one another for the emergency exits. The other hijacker, having been thrown down the aisle in the jolt, was picking himself up and preparing to beat a retreat when he spotted Harry, behind the Magnum, bursting through the first-class archway.

"Sit down, goddamnit," Harry yelled at the passengers.

The hijacker raised his pistol and popped off a wild shot, which ricocheted near Harry. He ducked. The hijacker then darted around and sought refuge in the restroom, pulling the door shut behind him. Without hesitation, Harry unleashed two shots, which traveled the length of the plane and caved in the restroom door. When the door dropped from its hinges, a very dead hijacker fell forward into the aisle.

Without so much as giving the man a second look, Harry turned and walked to the door of the plane. When he opened it, he was somewhat startled to see himself surrounded by a ring of police sharpshooters, ambulances, squad cars and fire trucks. A car came screeching up the runway, its siren blaring. It stopped abruptly and from a rear door Detective Lieutenant Neil Briggs rushed out. He looked up at the plane. Seeing Harry smiling in pilot's regalia, his mouth dropped open.

"Calahan, goddamnit, what are you doing here?" he shouted. But the cheering and applause of other onlookers drowned him out.

Chapter 6

Harry Calahan wheeled his Chevy into the parking lot behind the police building. It was his first free night in two weeks and he was eagerly anticipating using the time to get himself back into shape for the upcoming annual target-shooting championship sponsored by the Police Benevolent Association. Of the dozen years Harry had been with the San Francisco police force, there were very few in which he did not walk away with the bulkiest trophies from these contests. In fact, there was only one year—1967—when he won none of the events, but that was only because he had been unable to enter the contest that year. The reason for his abstention was a splintered pinkie on his trigger hand, an injury sustained in combat that summer in the Haight district with a psychotic, acid-crazed, knife-freak runaway from Mineola, Long Island. Not since then had Harry Calahan been so ill prepared for the P.B.A. shoot-offs as he felt he was this year.

He was in his third month on loan to the stakeout squad, a diversion he would not normally have welcomed even for a day, which was all the loan had been intended for—until the vindictive Briggs had decided to turn it into an extended tour. For a cop like Harry, the stakeout squad was tantamount to being sent to Siberia. Guns, like musical instruments, require a good deal of practice before one can gain and then maintain the skills it takes to play them just right, and stakeout wasn't much of a place for on-the-job opportunities in this regard. The stakeout squad meant just that—staking out, sometimes for days on end, with nothing to do but take turns napping and watching. In Homicide, Harry had grown used to a great many more in-the-line-of-duty chances for target practice than the present somnolent assignment could or would ever offer.

In fact, other than the one occasion on which he'd foiled the hijacking, Harry hadn't used his gun once in three months. As he drove up and down the parking lot looking for an available space in which to deposit his car, he wondered how much longer he'd have to suffer stakeout before Briggs finally relented and put him back in the action, where he belonged. He was more than well aware that it didn't take long for a man to grow rusty. Especially with a Magnum.

He found a parking place, locked the car, and retrieved a bag of pistol equipment from the trunk. With the bag swinging from his hand, he walked toward a series of stairs at the far end of the police building. The metal stairs led down into a subterranean pistol range.

It was a cool, clear, spring night, and the wind was blowing an unseasonal chill as Harry huddled in a nylon windbreaker to conserve his body warmth. On the way to the stairs he passed by a line of blue and white motorcycles which belonged to Traffic. He stared at the machines gleaming under the overhead fluorescent streetlamps, and frowned. As he had done so many times in the previous ten days, he searched and searched again in his mind for some new angle in the Ricca murder. All there seemed to be was the driver's license with the bullet hole. This had led Harry to believe that whoever the killer was, he had posed as a motorcycle cop—that is, if, in fact, he was *not* a motorcycle cop, which was not as remote a possibility as Harry preferred to believe it was.

Suddenly, in the midst of reconstructing the Ricca killing for what must have been the nth time, he heard a set of tires screeching behind him. It sounded a little too close, so he pitched himself out of the way and holed up between two parked cars that appeared to belong to civilians but were actually unmarked official vehicles. The screeching changed to a sound of metal scraping metal. Harry turned and spotted a white late-model Ford ramming its way through a narrow space between two parked cars, causing them damage far in excess of normal supermarket scratches. Harry tried for a look at the driver, but the light was insufficient. His curiosity, as usual, undeterred, he sought a better perspective. Finding one, he discovered with a mixture of fascination and shock that the driver was none other than Charlie McCoy, the second-best shot on the force (though doomed to Traffic for his entire career) and a longtime pal of Harry's, if not his most long-standing friend in the department. Charlie's face was twisted into some half-mad, half-stoned contortion. He was wheeling hard, standing on the gas pedal, severely denting all three cars. He finally broke through, but only at the cost of picking up two extra bumpers on the way. Clouds of smoke billowed from his Ford's tires.

Harry stepped out, waving, but McCoy, failing to see him, aimed the car straight at him. For one brief moment —as he caught a glimpse of saliva bubbles collecting on Charlie McCoy's lips—it looked like sure ironic death for Dirty Harry. In fact, it was only inches away when the car skidded to a sliding stop. McCoy, dressed in his motorcycle officer's gear and boots, lurched out through the door and charged blindly at Harry.

"Hello, Charlie," Harry said as casually as a man would greet his neighbor at the corner bus stop.

McCoy halted abruptly. He did a double take at the sound of his name, squinted, and then resorted to a pair of unsightly glasses. These abetted him in recognizing that the man greeting him was his old pal, Harry Calahan, and no sooner did this realization come than he broke out in a full, effusive belly laugh.

Harry also laughed, though in a slightly more constrained manner. He obviously felt mixed emotions about running into his pal under these peculiar circumstances.

"Harry! You crazy son of a bitch you, I could have killed you!" McCoy finally said through the last sputters of his laugh. Harry found himself wondering whether, in fact, Charlie had intended to kill him before he realized who he was. McCoy extended both arms and took Harry in a bear hug, slapping him at the same time, showing much masculine affection. Harry put his pistol bag on the ground and smiled. The affection was undoubtedly mutual, though Harry obviously would have preferred running into his old friend in a more figurative manner. Nonetheless he was pleased to see him.

"How are you, Charlie?"

"Harry, I haven't seen you in a coon's age and maybe longer."

"Been that long?" Harry stroked his chin.

"If not longer."

"I've been meaning to stop by one night," Harry explained, full of guilt. "How's Carol?"

"I don't live with the old lady anymore, Harry. Not for five months now."

"I'm sorry to hear that, Charlie," Harry offered. It was the best he could do. He was not eager for the details. "I've been busy. You know how it is."

"I know all about you Homicide boys."

"Briggs has me on stakeout these days. That's the problem."

But Charlie failed to hear. "Carol was my third time at bat, Harry," he said.

Harry shook his head sadly. Charlie paused in the silence, his eyes abstracted and staring off into nowhere. He held the daze for a few moments, much to Harry's fascination, and then broke out of it, wondering aloud, "Where does time go, Harry?"

"That's a very good question, Charlie."

"You know, I'm afraid of time." Charlie shifted his tone lower. "I know you ten years now, Harry, do you realize that? Ever since I came out here. Something to think about, huh?"

"Yeh."

"You don't look older to me, though. Tell me, Harry, do I look older to you?"

Harry did not answer directly, partly because Charlie did indeed look older—some *twenty* years older, as a matter of fact—and partly because it was getting late and he was anxious to get to the pistol range. So, in the interests of conserving time and small talk, he tightened his jaw and said: "Maybe you shouldn't really be out on the streets anymore, Charlie."

38

"What do you mean by that? You do think I'm getting older, don't you?"

"That's not what I said. I *said* maybe you shouldn't—"

"Harry, we should have put our twenty in the Marines," Charlie interrupted, shaking his head regretfully. "With the way things are these days, a cop kills a hoodlum on the street, he's better off dumping the body in a river than he is reporting it. Those snot-nosed young bastards in the D.A.'s office crucify you one way or the other. Only the criminals got rights, not us. What's this fucking country coming to? Do you ever think about that, Harry? I think about it all the time. They got this idea here where a hood can kill a cop and get off without so much as a night in the can, but let a cop go and kill a hood and the whole world's crying 'police brutality.' Am I right, Harry?"

"Charlie, why don't you think about it? Take an early retirement."

To reply, Charlie leaned in close, indicating that he was about to reveal something of the utmost secrecy.

"I know you ten years, Harry, so I'll tell you something just between you and me," he confided eagerly. His face had taken on an angry scowl. "I'll never retire! There's only one way I'm going out—and that's fucking. Fucking and fighting, that's how. That's all there is anyway." Harry remained unblinking even as Charlie tossed on this searching epilogue: "Am I right?"

Unable to find any words for a suitable reply, Harry nodded noncommittally, tapped his old pal on the shoulder and headed into the building.

Chapter 7

A bag of pistol equipment in hand, Harry Calahan raced down the steps and through a darkened hallway to the underground pistol range. It was almost ten o'clock. The encounter with Charlie McCoy, aside from upsetting him, had delayed him for fifteen minutes. Not that Harry was operating on any sort of schedule, but he was due to report the following morning at four for another innocuous stakeout in North Beach, and he liked to get at least seven hours' sleep each night, whenever possible. As he walked down the corridor he heard only the sound of his own footsteps, but then as he turned in the doorway to the range he heard—and saw—a target silhouette of a man with a mask and a gun pop up at the far end of the room. Three rapid-fire shots went off and the target, drilled dead center, popped back down. At this hour the range was normally deserted, and it disturbed Harry immensely that on this night, of all nights, it wasn't.

As another set of targets loomed up in pools of light, he stepped into the darkened, sprawling, low-ceilinged catacombs. Four young men turned and surveyed him. They all wore embroidered workshirts, faded jean and boots, and looked far more indigenous to a college campus than an underground pistol range. Only their shoulder holsters gave away the difference. Seeing Harry, they all smiled. But Harry refrained from any such pleasantries. Figuring the men for recent recruits, he regarded them coldly. He was put off by their style and their age. Harry was not from the school that thought a good cop had to have a college education, and he didn't like the fact that the department had in recent years put a great deal of emphasis on campus recruiting.

"You boys rookies?" he demanded.

40

The tallest of the four young men nodded, adjusting the glasses on the bridge of his nose. He was an extremely rugged-looking type, blond, large in frame, with penetrating blue eyes. He reached to shake Harry's hand, but Harry ignored him.

"I'm Ben Davis," the young man said, unfazed. "Patrolman, Traffic. That's Phil Sweet, John Grimes and Red Astrachan. We're all rookies. You're Inspector Harry Calahan, right?"

Harry nodded, still refusing Davis's hand.

"We've heard a lot about you," Davis offered with obvious admiration.

But Harry only wanted to know: "What are you doing here at this hour?"

"Just practicing, sir," Davis replied.

"Don't you have regular classes for this sort of thing?"

"Yes—on Monday nights."

But John Grimes, with his wire-rimmed glasses and long commonplace face, appearing to be the most intellectual and the least obtrusive of the lot, saw that Davis had missed the point. He explained, "As you know, Inspector Calahan, a cop shouldn't even be on the street today if he can't shoot well. Killers don't make allowances."

It was an argument to which Harry Calahan could only be sympathetic. "I can't fault you there," he relented. Then, shaking his head with chagrin, he took a place farther down on the firing line and removed the awesome .44 Magnum from his pistol bag. He had nothing more to say to the four young men.

However, Phil Sweet, the shortest of the four—he had a roundish, cherubic, bespectacled face and looked barely twenty-one years old—welled up with something akin to hero worship and couldn't contain himself from asking, "Sir, are you shooting in the combat championship next week?"

"I always do." Harry turned, annoyed at the small talk. "Why?"

Red Astrachan grinned. He was tall, loose and outgoing, and, if his face was any indication, had the best sense of humor. "You win every year, Mr. Calahan. It's become sort of an institution around here," he said.

Harry, still uninterested, loaded his gun.

"You're a living legend," Grimes told him.

All this adulation seemed to have little effect. Harry remained irritated. Half to himself, half to the others, he muttered, "There's no other time I can get this place alone."

Davis heard the remark, and offered, accommodatingly: "We'll leave if you want the range to yourself. No problem."

Harry was on the verge of accepting this proposition when he sunk a tooth into his lip and reconsidered. They wouldn't get in his way, he decided, and he did appreciate their attitude.

"No, you can stay," he allowed, pushing a button at the end of a cord to set up the targets. "But I like to set up my own routines."

The targets which were already standing retreated and new ones appeared in a somewhat different arrangement, turned at angles so as to further diminish the vital target areas. Harry liked things difficult—in life and in target practice. He was a man challenged by circumstances; the more challenging the circumstances, the more adroit and efficient his response.

All four patrolmen stopped to watch with intense interest. Harry, however, continued to pay them no attention. He again pushed the button, retracting the targets. He always checked mechanical equipment before relying on it. Then he took a place on the firing line, furrowed his brow and loaded a cylinder into the gun. It locked in place with a smooth click, and he removed another plastic cylinder, loaded with .44 bullets, and placed it on a stand near him.

"Sir, what kind of load are you using there?" Sweet inquired.

Harry, elaborately annoyed by the interruption, turned fiercely to say, "If it means anything to you, Sweet, I'm using a light .44 Special—no recoil, and with the weight of this gun, I've got more control than a .357 even with

42

light wad cutters. Now, Sweet, are there any more questions, because it's getting late."

"No sir, sorry." Sweet smiled. He and the others donned pairs of noise-suppressing earphones. Harry also put on a pair himself and then turned around to push the starter button. Even before the targets were in full operation, he wheeled back, fell to his knee, gun drawn in his left hand, and fired. The noise was deafening; a Magnum sounds as fierce as it looks. A target went down with a center shot. Then Harry, eyes wide, pulled the recoil again and blasted several more shots, the flame spitting out of the barrel of his gun. One target after another dropped, almost in rhythm. The four young men looked on in astonishment, realizing for the first time that Dirty Harry, as they, like everybody else, privately called him, fully deserved every superlative attached to his reputation.

Harry blasted two more shots, spinning behind the barrier, reaching for the next plastic cylinder with his right hand.

When the firing stopped, all the targets were down. The stakeout squad hadn't taken as much a toll on his skill as he had feared it had, and it pleased him.

He glanced at the quartet of patrolmen, looking for a response. But the men seemed to him, for some peculiar reason, less responsive in expressing their adulation than he figured they should have been. Somewhat less than noticeably irritated, Harry jammed the next plastic cylinder into the Magnum, spun the cartridge, pressed the target set-up button and came out shooting rapid-fire from behind the barrier. Again, all the targets were felled, this time in an even more speedy, rhythmic succession. It was a magnificent performance, equal to any he'd ever staged.

This time the four young patrolmen all nodded appreciatively. Harry rose from his knee, removed the noise suppressants from his ears and placed the smoking Magnum on the stand. He picked Sweet's face to look into because it held the least expression.

"Like to try it?" Harry asked him.

"No sir, I don't believe I would," Sweet replied.

43

"Go ahead," Harry challenged, grinning.

"No, I don't think so."

"Go on," Harry insisted. "You'll never know what you're like until you try it." He opened the cylinder and handed the Magnum to the youth.

"Well, okay."

Sweet took the gun, handling it as gently and confidently as a mother would handle her infant child. He held it for a moment in one hand, examining it closely, then hefted it once to feel the weight. He found it very heavy, marveling, "Gee." After looking into the assenting eyes of his three friends, he removed his horn-rimmed glasses, apologizing, "I'm farsighted."

Again he put on the ear plugs and loaded and holstered the gun. He limbered both arms like an Olympic swimmer before a race, wiping his hands on his jeans. Harry was amused by the elaborate preparations. A thin smile crept over his lips.

Sweet nodded to Davis and Davis pressed the button to snap up Harry's last set of targets. Suddenly Sweet's eyes came wide open. He whipped the gun from the holster and blasted six bullets so incredibly fast that they resounded almost like a single shot. When he finished he pulled the smoking gun out of recoil. All the targets were down.

Harry was speechless and amazed.

Sweet squinted three or four times--and reloaded expertly with another speedloader. Davis again hit the button, this time unable to conceal a slight grin. Sweet's gun roared, drilling all the targets dead center except for one, which was left standing. He pulled out the ear plugs and wiped his brow.

"It's just a bit too heavy for me," Sweet lamented, handing the gun back to Harry, the cylinder open. "I missed one."

Harry replied generously, "Well, Sweet, nobody's perfect, you know."

"Guess not."

"Tell me something, Sweet. You didn't learn to shoot like that around here?"

"Airborne—Rangers, Special Forces, sir." Sweet put on his glasses again.

"Yeh." Harry shrugged. "Well, I can see how that might help some. When were you discharged?"

"A couple of months ago, sir."

"How about the rest of you guys?" Harry wanted to know. "Are you even *close?*"

Sweet answered for them. "Grimes is dog nuts—about even with me. Astrachan is a little better. Davis is a lot, an awful lot, better."

Grimes smiled and punched Astrachan on the shoulder, Astrachan smiled and punched Davis on the shoulder, Davis smiled and punched Sweet on the shoulder. The performance made Harry wonder aloud: "Were you fellas in the service together?"

"Yes, sir," four times.

Harry, getting back to what Sweet had said, bellowed, "Better! Davis is better! One thing for sure, Sweet, you do have a sense of style. I'll give you that! *Better!*"

The four patrolmen laughed.

Unable to restrain himself any further, Harry shook his head approvingly and broke into a huge happy grin.

"When I get back on my next homicide assignment, you guys come and see me," he said. With that he shook their hands. Astrachan took a poke at Grimes, who sidestepped, and clipped his nose. They all laughed.

"I'm glad we finally had a chance to meet you, sir." Davis was the spokesman.

Harry nodded, feeling very light, very good.

Chapter 8

Situated a dozen or so miles north of the Golden Gate Bridge, the Tiburon peninsula juts eastward into San Francisco Bay, offering magnificent vistas of the bay area from its countless coves and hillsides. To the northwest, over the rolling hills that turn from green in winter to brown in summer, towers the majestic Mount Tamalpais, where canyons of redwood groves lie below chaparral-blanketed ridges. In the sinuous curves of its slopes the Indians saw a gracefully reclining woman's body and dubbed the mountain "The Sleeping Maiden." To the east and across the bay lies Oakland, thick in urban sprawl, and in the distance, the awesome Mount Diablo. South, between the Golden Gate and Bay bridges, lies that shining city of cities, San Francisco, whose otherwise charming skyline is dominated by a twenty-first century pyramid which serves as home office for an insurance company, and by another, more conventional, boxlike skyscraper which houses California's largest bank.

At the very tip of the Tiburon peninsula, through the Racoon Straits, Angel Island rises from the bay as a lush green mountain. Several miles farther on, toward the city, is yet another island, this one perhaps more well known to most people: Alcatraz. Both these islands represent two aspects of life in the bay area: its awesome beauty and its longtime troublesome affiliation with violence and lawlessness, marking it at least in one respect as no different from America's other urban areas.

Though both islands can be viewed from certain perspectives on the Tiburon, it is the more ethereal Angel Island to which the peninsula reaches out, in spirit and in fact. Tiburon, its hills abounding with estates, its coves cluttered with sailboats, is a very peaceful place whose inhabitants spend working days in the cities, many of them commuting by ferry, some by limousine. Some have limousines and don't commute at all. The peninsula is made up of two very uncrowded towns, Tiburon and Belvedere, each nothing more than a small village circled by hills resplendent with foliage and beautiful, expensive homes.

On a warm and windless late-spring afternoon, the day after Harry Calahan had the strange encounter with his old friend Charlie McCoy, a large figure crouched on a bare Tiburon hillside, staring down hard at a huge Georgian mansion several hundred feet below. The mansion was surrounded by a stone wall. A driveway snaked through a row of eucalyptus trees to a gate, beyond which a virtual fleet of Mercedes, Cadillacs and Lincoln Continentals were parked. The grounds were well-tended and dazzled with blooming flowers.

The figure squatting on the hillside, though obscured by the sun at his shoulder, appeared to be a man dressed as a police officer. He was not visible from the mansion below. He unlimbered a satchel from his shoulder, gently setting it on the ground. Then he raised and loaded an M-16 rifle, falling to one knee to focus the telescopic sight on the activity taking place on a patio surrounding an Olympic-size swimming pool.

The gunsight fell on a blond woman wearing an extremely brief yellow polka-dot bikini. She got up from a lounge chair and walked, missing no opportunity to swing her behind, to the diving board. Her strut magnetized most eyes in the immediate pool area. On one finger she wore an enormous diamond, which glittered in the sunshine. She reached the diving board, looked around, and smiled.

"Okay, baby, let's see it!" came the gruff voice of one of the men at poolside. "Show us how nice you can do it."

The blond blinked several times and undulated. Her undulation was a gesture every bit as obscene as any seen in a soft-core porno flick, no less (nor more) inviting. The man crouching on the hillside with the gun winced, squirmed, and coughed uncomfortably. The sight of the blond had somewhat unsettled certain regions of his body.

47

However, he was able to cool off, if only vicariously, as she limbered one final time and took a swan dive into the pool, disappearing momentarily under the water.

At poolside sat about a half dozen men, all stocky or bulky, in bathing suits. Several smoked cigars, which they unplugged from their mouths when they had something to say, and plugged back in when they finished. In addition to the men were a half dozen women, all scantily attired and gorgeous. The women did not, to the naked eye, appear to be the men's wives. The scene, in all its hedonistic splendor, would have been equally appropriate were it taking place on the French Riviera.

One of the men, heavy-jawed and flabby-faced, sat with his legs in the pool, draining the last of a drink. He finished it down to and including the ice cubes, and set the glass down. The laughter, animated conversation and tinkling ice cubes were well out of earshot of the man with the gun squatting on the hillside, who upon the blond's descent underwater had refocused his attention and telescopic sight on a heavyset Italian man with a commanding demeanor (undoubtedly the host) who in that instant appeared in the doorway to the patio, surveyed the scene, and then began ambling through, greeting everybody amiably. Everybody treated him with the utmost casual deference.

Suddenly the blond emerged from underwater, and the manner in which she did so caused something of a stir. The men broke into a chorus of whistles, hoots and cheers.

"Come on, baby, let's see more!"

"Atta girl!"

"Good show, baby!"

What enthralled them, of course, was the sudden absence of her bikini top. It wasn't entirely clear whether glorious self-exposure was accidental or intentional until she gave it away by calling: "Come on. Now, let's all go naked."

Her voice was high and eager.

"Put that goddamned top back on!" The heavyset host became livid, thrashing his forefinger through the air at the blond. "Hey, you guys, don't look at her! Look at me! Get your eyes off her! I catch anybody looking at her and I kill them!"

The six men laughed with nervous respect and reeled their heads in other directions. The blond quickly replaced the top, her eyes full of apologies. The host was clearly not a man to be defied.

On the hillside the sun reflected on the barrel of the M-16 as the man set it on the ground. He then lifted the satchel with both hands, one on bottom and one on top, quickly pulled a cord and lobbed the bag down to the patio. Smoke billowing into the air as it descended, the satchel hit the pool, splashing into the water barely an arm's length away from the blond. She jerked back in horror.

The men around the pool scrambled to their feet, reaching for their guns. When they all turned to look up at the hillside, the gunman opened up full automatic, his shots kicking up water all over the patio, shattering windows. One man fell, gushing blood, into the pool. The blond screamed as the water around her turned red. Hats bobbed everywhere.

A heavy-jawed man grabbed his legs as they were shot out from under him.

"Take cover, you fools," the hefty Italian host shouted wildly. He was running back toward the house when a series of bullets ripped through him.

Another man got it in the gut. He spit out a mouthful of ice cubes on his way down.

Suddenly the entire pool went up in a huge geyser as the plastic explosive went off, sounding like a depth charge. The concussion blew out all the remaining windows in the house. Moments later, the last of the moans and shattering glass were heard, and the scene fell still.

The man on the hillside, who'd been momentarily knocked off balance by the gun, picked himself up rapidly and dusted off. In so doing he dropped a pair of eyeglasses, retrieved them quickly, and darted off down a fire road to where he'd parked his motorcycle.

Chapter 9

Harry Calahan picked up off the TV set a framed photograph of Charlie McCoy. He was looking at it when, from the corner of his eye, he saw Briggs appear on the TV screen, emerging from a Georgian mansion in Tiburon. The lieutenant was followed by a half dozen detectives, an equal number of uniformed policemen and a horde of press and television reporters.

"Do you expect more underworld violence like this?" one of the reporters, on the run, called after Briggs.

"I have nothing to say at this time," was Briggs's comment. He did not stop walking.

A second reporter, also running, tried asking: "Is this gang war, lieutenant?"

Briggs, still refusing to slow, replied hotly: "This is not Chicago! This is San Francisco!"

Yet another reporter scrambled in Briggs's path, heading him off. He asked sardonically, "Sir, there were over fourteen hundred murders in San Francisco last year. Would you care to comment on that?"

A close-up of Briggs filled the television screen. He was scowling angrily. He managed some sort of sharp reply, but Harry Calahan could not hear precisely what it was through the screams and giggles of children playing in the room.

"Children! Behave yourselves!" came a woman's voice from the kitchen, but the children failed to heed the order. Harry continued to watch the screen intently as the camera panned to a police helicopter flying low over the mansion and then to a knot of ballistics men at work on a nearby hillside. Finally, as Briggs was getting into his car, another reporter managed this question: "Lieutenant,

50

do you think this mass murder signals open warfare in the Mafia?"

Briggs looked squarely into the camera. "There's going to be no more bombs in pools," he said fiercely. "This town belongs to the people. Now that's all I have to say at this time."

Harry clicked off the TV set and glanced one more time at Charlie McCoy's photograph before setting it down. As Briggs dwindled to a pinpoint of light, Harry's face locked into an extremely pensive expression, which he held for several long moments in spite of the two small boys and a little girl tumbling around him, shrieking, "Harry! Harry! Harry." Eventually, through their unyielding persistence, the children managed to tug him to the couch, where the little girl jumped to his knee. While Harry continued to stare blankly into the now-blank screen, she asked, wide-eyed and perspiring, "Do you like our dance, Harry, huh?"

Harry smiled at her from what might as well have been a million miles away.

"Huh, Harry, huh?"

"Huh what?"

"Do you like our dance?"

He flicked her cheek with his finger. He said: "It was very good."

The little girl grinned inscrutably and then leaped off Harry's lap to join her brothers again. This time they pretended to be little Indians hooting and dancing around a wagon train.

"I see you're really getting the full treatment tonight, Harry."

Carol McCoy, a pot of coffee in hand, appeared in the doorway from the kitchen. She was an attractive though plain-featured woman in her early thirties. The children continued their war dance, unperturbed by her presence. She smiled, not seeming to mind the pandemonium, entered the room and poured the coffee. She was not dressed in a manner that a woman normally dresses on normal occasions in her own home, but had done herself up rather ravishingly, and with care, in a pantsuit outfit and

51

perfectly coiffured hair, which she wore in a bun. She had obviously invested a great deal of effort in her appearance, though there was still an air about her that suggested some unspoken preoccupation.

"I haven't had a real good sit-down dinner like this in a long time, Carol," Harry said, grinning as she took a place neither too close nor too far from him on the couch. "And I sure liked the way you fixed those potatoes. How's that called again?"

"Au gratin."

"They don't serve 'em like that in the places I usually eat," Harry remarked.

"Where do you normally eat these days, Harry?"

"Oh—on the run, I guess. Wherever I can."

The children, deprived of attention, came back to Harry, tugging again. The little girl insisted: "Harry, Harry, come dance with us!"

Harry smiled and lifted the girl up by her armpits. Carol clapped her hands and intervened sternly, "All right, kids, that's enough now. Say good night to Harry—and off to bed."

Harry put the girl back down on the floor. She and her brothers grumbled about having to say good night, but with some further persuasion Carol was able to convince them it was past their bedtime. The younger of the two boys gave Harry a hug, the older followed with a handshake. The girl closed her eyes and kissed him. He smiled and messed her hair.

"Come on now, children, bedtime!" Carol insisted.

The three children ran from the room, the smallest boy chewing on the bottom of his shirt, which was pulled up over his stomach.

"Take that out of your mouth, Richard," Carol shouted. For the first time there was some genuine annoyance in her voice, the source of which she explained to Harry as: "Sometimes they're just a little too much for me. I can't afford a woman coming in anymore."

"You seem to manage very well," Harry reassured her.

"Yeh, I just laugh all day long," Carol laughed, relieving herself. She straightened up on the couch, catching

52

Harry coquettishly in the corner of her eye. After a pause, she moved a few inches closer and said through nervous lips, "I'm glad you called, Harry. I really am."

"Yeh. It's been a long time, hasn't it?"

"Sure has, Harry."

"You don't look any worse for it, Carol."

"You either, Harry."

"Sometimes I feel like I'm getting old."

"Oh come on, Harry. You won't be old till the day you die, if I know you."

He enjoyed her way of putting it, and showed this by scratching playfully between his narrow deep-set blue-gray eyes. A lamp on an end table set his face in a series of shadows, darkening areas around his nose, chin and eyes. He was amused by her comment, his thin lips becoming even thinner as they pressed together and curled up at the edges. He looked at her fondly.

"Are you working?" he asked.

"Off and on, part time. At Sears."

"Does Charlie send you any money?"

"Sometimes, but I don't count on it."

Harry shook his head sadly. With his mention of Charlie, the tone of things shifted somewhat. Carol squirmed uncomfortably. Her eyes took one long blink.

"Carol?"

"Yes?"

"Have you seen Charlie lately?"

Carol reached over and picked up a toy fire engine on the floor near her foot. She smiled painfully, swallowing without opening her mouth. Then she exhaled and began chewing on her thumb. When she realized what she was doing, she stopped abruptly.

Finally, she managed, "More coffee, Harry?"

"Sorry," Harry said sincerely.

"It's hard for me to talk about it," she admitted.

"It's okay."

"No, really, I should tell you."

"Not if you don't want to, Carol."

"I saw Charlie last night. He said he wanted to come over and see the kids." She blurted this out and then

53

stopped suddenly to plummet into a long silence. Harry reached over and touched her shoulder, offering reassurance. He dipped his head down to catch her eyes, then held them.

"Oh, Harry, it's so hard."

"What happened, Carol?"

She raised her eyes sadly. The sadness made her even more attractive, showing her strength. She began to play with her hair and then reached for a cigarette. Harry lit it for her.

He looked at her as if to softly say, "Well?" but his lips remained steady. The smile had lost gaiety and turned to compassion. He nodded and said finally, "Why don't you tell me, Carol."

"He tried to jump out that window over there, Harry."

When the full impact of her words struck him he could only shake his head speechlessly. He turned to look again at Charlie's photo on the TV, then to the window. He gazed through it, his face screwed up in concern.

"What happened?" he asked eventually.

"I've been thinking about it over and over all day long and I'm still not sure."

"Try, Carol."

"When he came in he seemed fine. Then he wanted to, uh, you know, but I wouldn't. I just didn't want to . . ."

"Is that why he tried to jump?"

"I don't think so, Harry. He was upset for a while, but then when I went into the kitchen to make dinner, he began playing with the kids and it seemed like he'd forgotten. But I don't know." She was using a great deal of effort to hold back tears.

Harry stroked her head.

She managed a forced smile, but her eyes grew moist.

"Things happen," Harry said. "Sometimes you can't explain them."

"It was after we finished dinner when he tried it. I asked him about his job and he turned white and started screaming about how criminals are taking over the city, and that the law was protecting them. He told me about some gangster who was murdered and said that was the

54

best thing that happened all year and that there was going to be a lot more of it. He had this very strange look in his eye, Harry, and it frightened me. He just stared at me and breathed real heavily and I began to cry."

"Is that when he did it?"

"Yes. He walked over to the window. I thought he was just going to open it for some air and then he started crawling through."

"Jesus."

"I went up and pulled him back and started screaming. Then the people next door heard me screaming and came in to help. Finally we were all able to coax him out of it." She was shaking with every word until finally she fell apart, sobbing, "Harry, what do you tell children when they ask you why their father tried to jump out the window?"

He took her head in his hands and dried her tears with his handkerchief. "What did you tell them, Carol?"

"I told them it was a special kind of sickness that some people have. They wanted to know if it was a kind of sickness that you can get better from. I told them that yes, there were doctors who could cure it. As if that were true."

"Carol," Harry said, pausing, "do you know where Charlie is living now?"

She collected herself, grief turning into anger. "I don't know and I don't care!"

"Carol."

"Harry, he's a sick man. He shouldn't be allowed to carry a gun anymore, if you want my opinion."

"Do you know where he's living?"

She did not want to show that she did, but finally relented to Harry's inquisitive eyes. "The last I heard he was living on Nob Hill somewhere—with one of those nude dancing girls from North Beach." She interrupted herself to laugh hysterically. When she quieted down, she announced, "Well, I'm over that. I have to survive too."

But it was evident to Harry that Carol McCoy was not entirely over it. Nonetheless, he assured her, referring to her comment about survival, "You will."

It gave her strength to see that he agreed. Recomposing herself, she dropped back onto the couch, closing in a few inches on him. She did not leave an altogether healthy distance between them. Harry, noting this, awkwardly shifted in place. Then she moved even closer. Staring heavily, she spoke: "Harry, if I ask you something personal would you mind?"

"I know Charlie ten years," was Harry's diplomatic reply to the anticipated question.

"Charlie has nothing to do with this anymore, Harry."

"Ten years, Carol. That makes him an old friend."

"You know me seven, Harry. That makes us old friends too, doesn't it?"

"Sure."

"Well then, do you mind if I ask you?" She moved her head close to his as she spoke.

"If you want."

She gathered the words on her lips and then shot them out: "Harry, how come you never made a pass at me?"

Harry gulped. The room fell silent. He looked at the window, then at Charlie's photograph. Carol chased his eyes, and then abruptly took his hand and put it on her breast. For a moment he froze. Carol moved closer, and was about to kiss him when a shriek came from the bedroom.

"Mommmmmmmmmmieeeeeeeee!" It was the little girl. In the midst of her shrieking came the sound of something crashing and shattering.

"My God!" Carol uttered from between her teeth. "With those kids, do you think I'll ever get laid?"

She stalked into the bedroom and came back in a few moments, explaining, "She knocked over a lamp. I guess I'm really on edge."

Harry, relieved by the little girl's timely interference, consoled: "You got good reason, Carol." He followed this with a laugh. She mistook the lightness in his tone as a cue to resume, and reached to stroke his hair. He did not seem to know how to respond when the telephone saved him from making the decision.

Carol shook her head in frustration and went to answer

it. "Yes," she said, "he's here. One minute." She nodded to Harry with disappointed eyes. "It's for you," she sighed.

Calahan got up and took the receiver. "Yeh? . . . I thought we were off tonight, Smith. . . . Yeh, uh huh. . . . Okay, okay, I'll be right there. I'll be coming in the back way."

When Harry put the phone down, Carol stood up and said, without bitterness, "Good night, Harry." He frowned and she followed him to the door, where she kissed him a more elaborate than usual old-friends' kiss. Harry gently removed himself, saying, "You did me an honor, Carol. I want you to know that. I mean it." Then he left.

In the hallway he smiled sadly, and let out a long breath. While waiting for the elevator he checked to see that his .44 Magnum was in good order.

Chapter 10

Less than ten minutes after leaving Carol McCoy's place, Harry Calahan arrived at the destination to which he'd been summoned—a discount store in the Fillmore district. He pulled into a narrow alley that led to a loading area in the rear, where he abandoned the car and slipped into the building through a back door. He proceeded hurriedly through storage quarters to a second door, which opened into the sales area of the store.

He cracked the door open half an inch and saw his partner, Early Smith, a short distance away, standing behind the counter in a stock boy's jacket. Next to Smith was the store's owner. He was a thick-set man who perspired heavily. The edges of his collar were turned up and his shirt was half in and half out of the trousers. He wore a tie which, from the way he kept shifting his neck, seemed to serve more as a self-strung noose than a sartorial adornment. In one of his eager looks around the store, the owner spotted Harry peering through the crack in the door. Harry nodded affirmatively at him, backing away a few inches.

A uniformed cop, wearing a bulletproof vest, was watching the store, with a gun ready, from the other side of a two-way mirror. Harry first noticed him when he backed away from the door.

"Over there by the magazine rack," the cop whispered to Harry. The reference was to a thin, tense-looking black-haired man who appeared to be browsing through *Time* Magazine, but was in fact glancing over it, trying to size up Early and the owner.

"What's the deal?" Harry whispered.

"Owner thinks he saw the guy just before the last robbery," the cop said without removing his eyes from the man.

"Hm," Harry said.

"Whaddya think?" the cop asked him.

"Well, he sure as hell don't look like a paying customer to me," Harry replied in a whisper. He studied the man closely through the mirror.

The cop laughed softly.

The store was crowded with evening shoppers. Looking through the two-way mirror, Harry found it possible to see all the way through the store to the front windows and beyond. He winced when he spotted a car parked across the street in a no-parking zone.

"That car," he whispered urgently to the cop. "Across the street! See it?"

"Jesus H. Christ!" The cop did all he could to keep his voice lowered, but was not altogether successful at it. "You're right! I didn't see it!"

Harry, with his jaw extended, gave the cop a what-the-hell's-the-matter-with-you look. He was angered at the man's myopia and loud mouth. "You didn't see it?" he asked finally, astonished.

"Nope."

"Get over there by the door with that shotgun," Harry said angrily, pointing.

As the cop started to do so, though none too quickly, he asked Harry, "You think it's a hit?"

Harry replied with hard-boiled eyes.

"Or a miss?" the cop, failing to note the eyes, continued.

Finally Harry just said in a loud whisper: "Hurry up!" The words were clipped and cold. He was obviously in no mood to hear the humor of an inept cop. The cop, finally sensing this, scrambled to the door.

"Now make sure you have that gun ready," Harry again told the cop, this time from his throat. He often spoke from his throat when he was angry. He turned from the cop back to the two-way mirror and saw some new and possibly foreboding activity taking place in the store. The thin man put *Time* down and started walking out,

59

passing three other men who were just entering. They all looked surreptitiously at one another.

One of the three men was tall and wiry, a second stocky, and the third, medium-size, was distinctive mostly for a coat draped over his arm. The stocky man took up a position at the door as the two others moved rapidly through the store. When they reached the counter where Early was standing with the owner, the tall man drew a handgun and the other man pulled the coat from his arm, exposing a sawed-off automatic shotgun. The owner's face drained of all color. Early's jaw tightened.

"Aw right—put 'em up!" the tall man demanded.

A woman, hearing the man's gruff voice, turned and saw the guns. She erupted in a full, uncontrollable scream. The man with the automatic slugged her with the butt of the gun, rendering her unconscious.

Harry whispered to Early through the two-way mirror: "Easy now. Stay loose."

All the shoppers in the front of the store froze as the man with the sawed-off automatic, looking up from the fallen woman, turned the gun on them.

"Christ!" the cop at the door whispered loudly to Harry. "What in the—what are we waiting for?" His finger twitched on the trigger.

"Shut up," Harry told him.

For good measure, the man with the shotgun kicked the woman on the floor; she showed signs of regaining consciousness. Early, seeing this, was unable to contain himself and grabbed for his piece under the counter. This prompted the tall man to level his handgun into the black inspector's face.

"Freeze, nigger!" he shouted. "Don't you go setting off no alarms or that's the end of your black ass."

Early froze. In doing so, without knowing it, he blocked Harry's view through the two-way mirror. Harry, who'd had his Magnum leveled directly at the tall man's heart, lowered it in disgust, swearing under his breath. Meanwhile, the cop at the door was all at loose ends, like a runner in a misstarted sprint.

"Keep still, asshole," Harry told him.

Though he could no longer see him, Harry heard the tall man, apparently talking to the owner, say: "Get over here, you! Fast!"

The owner, growing very jittery, went to the cash register.

"Now empty everything out of there into this sack," the tall man demanded. He tossed a cloth bag and waved his gun at the owner. When the owner hesitated for one brief and unfortunate second, the tall man rammed the barrel of the gun into his ribs.

A teenager who'd been standing near the magazine rack suddenly broke and ran for the door, but the man with the sawed-off shotgun stuck out a foot, tripped him, and proceeded to crack his skull with the gun. The teenager dropped spastically, bleeding. He rolled over and crashed into a pyramid display of detergent boxes.

The owner recovered quickly and set about rifling the cash register, as ordered. There was a puddle of sweat on his face when he finished stuffing all the bills into the sack.

"Now where's your safe, white nigger?" the tall man growled, grabbing the sack. "Hurry!"

"I, uh, haven't, uh, got a safe," the owner explained, but he was not very convincing.

"You lying sack of shit! Where is it, man?"

"Honest, I—"

"You got three seconds to tell me where that safe is!"

"Uh, I, uh . . ." The owner trembled and shut his eyes in prayer. The tall man, losing all patience, swung the gun, smashing him in the face. The owner staggered back and fell to the floor. Early, taking it all in, had such a difficult time containing himself that his whole body trembled from the effort.

"Okay, nigger," the tall man turned on him, "where's the safe?"

Early did not respond.

The man with the shotgun interceded, talking from the corner of his mouth, "Let me take care of this, Jack." He nodded for the tall man to turn and stand guard over the shoppers as he sneered and extended the shotgun to Early's sealed lips. "Okay, nigger, suck it!"

Early still did not respond.

In the storeroom Harry was all concentration, trying to aim the Magnum. But Early unwittingly continued to block a good view.

"Now?" the cop whispered urgently to Harry.

Harry nodded negatively and lowered the gun.

"But—" the cop protested.

Harry shot him a mean, intolerant glance.

"You don't suck it, nigger," the man with the shotgun warned Early, "and I'm gonna blow your head off. It'll be my pleasure." He shoved the gun's barrel into Early's teeth. "You got to three. One . . ."

Just as he started counting he spotted the owner attempting to pull himself up off the floor, his pudgy face splotched with blood and pieces of shattered glass falling from his eyeglasses. With eyes momentarily riveted on the merchant, the man with the shotgun continued, absently, after a few seconds' pause: "Two."

Early flinched.

The tall man raised half a hand of fingers, indicating that he wanted his accomplice to delay the countdown just a bit so that he could take a moment to have one more word with the owner. "Now, honk, are you sure you still ain't got no safe? Cuz next time I ask it, you ain't gonna be here to answer that question."

"Please," the owner pleaded, "I don't have a safe, believe me."

Meanwhile, the man with the shotgun remained preoccupied with his own obsessions. He told Early, "Now right here is where I kill myself a nigger. Get down on your knees, motherfucker."

As Early started to dip slowly, the tall man suddenly became visible to Harry, who smiled as he took his Magnum confidently in both hands. The blast of the gun shattered the two-way mirror and sent the tall man reeling back in a hail of glass.

Shoppers in the store started screaming and trampling over one another for the exits.

The cop burst through the door, shouting, "Hold it! Police!" to the man with the shotgun.

The man wheeled around and fired several shots at the cop. Though the bullets were rejected by his vest, they nonetheless knocked him off balance. Early leaped suddenly at the robber, but was repelled swiftly with a chop and a knee.

The man was about to finish Early off by shooting him point blank in the face when Harry burst through the shattered mirror, crouching low and firing. The robber managed to duck the shots, blasting back, then turned sharply and took off down an aisle.

Harry darted after him, slamming people and objects in his way. A terrified old lady scampering from his path caused him to momentarily lose sight of the man. He dusted off the woman with an immensely disgusted look. Then, spotting the third accomplice, the short man posted near the door, Harry raised his gun and blasted. The short man was blown backwards under the hard rain of a shattering plate-glass window. He managed to pick himself up to try a desperate dash for the getaway car across the street.

Early started after him, racing to the doorway, firing, but the man got to the car before the bullets could deter him.

Meantime, Harry again spotted the man with the shotgun, ducking low for cover near an elaborate cosmetics display. Approaching from behind, Harry raised his gun and aimed it carefully, but before he was able to get the shot off, the cop, up again, fired a wild shot with his service revolver. His bullet tore a hole through the bare stomach of a girl reclining in a life-size tanning-lotion display card.

The robber leaped up, pumping the gun, his bullets spraying through the store. He broke around the tanning-lotion display and headed for the door, inadvertently slamming into a display of deodorant cans stacked several feet high off the floor.

Early saw him and fired, plugging his arm. But the man, still far from dead, staggered ahead through the toppling cans, which began to explode one by one as they hit the floor.

Then Harry sighted him. He aimed. And fired. The man dropped the gun and fell backwards. The deodorant cans spun around him like hissing pinwheels.

The cop ran up, bracing. With two quick shots he finished off the robber. Having done so, the gun fell from his hand and he stood there trembling.

"I never killed a man before," he said softly, shaken.

"Yeh—that's pretty obvious," Harry snickered, very irritated. "You're not very good at it. You nearly got yourself and some of these other people here killed."

Early came running up. "The tall one over there is dead too, Harry," he said.

"Of course he is," Harry said. "I shot him."

It had just begun to rain when Harry Calahan and Early Smith pulled into the parking lot of the police building. Early was driving. Finding the lot crowded, he searched up and down several long rows for an available space. Neither he nor Harry had exchanged a single word since leaving the discount store. It was Early, finally finding a parking spot and cutting the motor, who broke the silence. He did so by whistling air through his mouth. It sounded like "Whew."

"You took that brush tonight okay," Harry told him.

Early shot back a leery, sidelong glance. "You work close, Harry!" he exclaimed. "Christ, do you work close."

"Only way to do it," Harry explained. "Besides, it makes it much more interesting."

They both got out of the car, leaving it unlocked. As they walked through the lot toward the building the headlights of another car illuminated four men in civilian clothes emerging from the building, carrying what appeared to be bowling bags. The men, all at once, looked up. Harry recognized them as Sweet, Davis, Astrachan and Grimes, the rookies he'd met several nights earlier at the combat range.

When they spotted him they waved.

Harry nodded, not all that enthusiastically. "Well, if it isn't the four musketeers," he muttered under his breath.

"Hey—where you guys off to?" Early called.

"Bowling," Davis said. "Castle Lanes over on Geneva Street."

Early waved as they passed. "Have a nice time," he said.

"You know those guys?" Harry asked.

"Them? Sure," Early said. "They're rookies. Traffic."

"What do you know about them?"

"They're like flypaper," Early said.

"Meaning?"

"Meaning they came through the academy together after me and I've never once seen them when they weren't together. We figure they must be queer for one another or something."

"Well, I'll tell you something, Smith," Harry said evenly. "If the rest of you guys could shoot like them, I wouldn't give a damn if the whole damned department was queer."

Chapter 11

It was raining heavily in San Francisco, though the night air was a little less chilly than usual. In front of the Fairmont Hotel, on a hill overlooking the city, a hysterical scene that typically occurs on such nights was in progress—people jockeying and fighting for the few available cabs.

A stunning black woman in her late twenties emerged, in a great hurry, through the revolving doors of the hotel. Every part of her sinuous body was in motion and heads swiveled from all corners to catch a glimpse of her and the brief mauve skirt and orange earrings she wore. She stood out in such striking incongruity to the otherwise stately milieu that she was as difficult not to look at as a solar eclipse.

She pulled off her shoes and hit the pavement, splashing by a line of people, dressed in full evening attire, all waiting for cabs. When she reached the head of the line, she muscled ahead of a man and woman who were about to step into the next cab. Before they even had a chance to react, the black woman palmed a bill into the doorman's practiced hands, and with her shoes under her arm jumped into the cab, and was gone. The crowd stood transfixed for a moment in the rain, then began swearing properly under their umbrellas. The doorman, poker-faced and oblivious, whistled for another cab.

The woman gave the cab driver an address in the Nob Hill district. Settling back, she pulled a wad of bills from between her half-exposed breasts. As she did this she found the driver's eyes, in the rear-view mirror, crawling all over her. She caught the eyes and held them tightly for a brief second. The driver started to say something to her, stopped, then tried again. When he finally got it out, it came mumbled under his breath, as if at the last minute he lost his courage and decided to say it to himself rather than to the woman.

"Huh?" the woman demanded, turning haughty.

The driver, a portly middle-aged man, strained to keep his tone matter-of-fact. He managed, "I said that money isn't everything." He sounded, in spite of himself, hopeful.

"Sheeeeit." The woman slouched back in the seat and began laughing insultingly.

"It isn't," the driver insisted.

"How would you know." It was not a question.

The driver gulped. He had a roundish face, several days unshaven.

"Sheeeeit," the woman said again.

"I mean it."

The woman counted the bills carefully and stuffed them back between her breasts, evidently pleased with the amount. She looked out the rain-splattered window, indicating that she did not care to hear any further taxicab aphorisms.

But the driver, not satisfied that he had made his point, went on: "There are other things in life."

The woman winced, as if that were the dumbest thing she'd ever heard. "What you talkin' about? You ever been poor, man?"

The driver sat up righteously, turned his head back and announced, "Fucking right I have. Poorer than you ever been!"

The woman did not accept the challenge. "Well, you sure as shit don't talk like it," she said, pulling her shoes on. This effectively ended the conversation. In a few minutes the cab reached its destination, a luxury apartment house on Lombard Street.

The woman, saying nothing, pushed a bill in the driver's face and stepped out of the cab, head down, hunched against the battering rain. Just as she turned to close the door her breath locked and she gasped. A huge black man wearing a fedora hat took her violently by the elbow and shoved her back into the cab. The driver whipped his neck around, his mouth gone slack. Once the woman was

67

back inside, writhing under the man's grip, the man himself, his blackness glistening from the rain, climbed in after her. He did not ease his hold, and she started moaning. He slapped her.

"Shut up, whore!" he said, closing the door behind him. He was wearing a sealskin Edwardian jacket. His upper lip twitched.

"Drive," he commanded the driver.

The driver, about to protest, changed his mind and substituted: "Where to?"

"Just keep making right turns until I tell you to stop. And drop that flag!"

"Right turns?" The driver hesitated a beat.

The pimp leaned forward, forming a nasty-looking fist.

"Yes sir!" said the driver, reacting quickly. He smacked the flag down and pulled away. At the corner he turned right down a steep hill without streetlights. The cab grew dark, except for the green lights from the dashboard.

"Let me go!" the woman screamed. The man had both his hands at her neck.

"You been holding out on me, bitch."

She replied with overly innocent eyes.

"Let's just see what's in the titty bank here," the pimp snickered. He took the liberty to explore for himself, but before his hand reached the bills the woman managed to shrink away.

She protested, "I ain't been holding back, Sidney, I been comin' on straight with you." She raised a hand to cover her cleavage.

The pimp grabbed both her arms with one hand and pinned them behind her. With his other hand he went back to plunge none too gently into the valley of her breasts. He came up with a fistful of crumpled bills.

"Well, well. Hello, Mr. Green," he exclaimed sardonically.

With the cab still moving, the woman struggled fiercely for the door. The pimp, freeing her arms, pulled her back and slammed her across the face. Her eyes blurred and she fell to the floor, whimpering. The driver, shooting repeated nervous glances into the rear-view mirror, was tongue-tied, terrified and drenched in sweat. The rain continued to beat hard on the roof of the cab.

The woman lay semiconscious on the seat. The pimp pulled her up by her hair, but only ended up with a wig in his hands. On a second try he took hold of the girl's short kinky hair and jerked her head back over his knee. Her mouth widened, and as she screamed the pimp removed a can of drain opener from his jacket and poured its contents into her mouth. Her arms went wide, thrashing the air, but the pimp held tightly until he finished draining every last drop of the stuff into her. She choked, gagged, and fell to the floor, her body wracking in violent spasms.

The driver's hands trembled on the wheel. He did not look around.

"Stop here!" the pimp ordered.

The cab screeched to a halt. The driver opened his door and bolted out into the rain.

"You're awful lucky, honky," the pimp yelled after him. "Cuz you were next." He got out of the cab, popped open an umbrella, adjusted his fedora, and strolled off in the rain.

The driver, hiding behind a tree across the street, watched the man disappear around the corner. Slowly and cautiously he made his way back to his cab, opened the back door, and found the black woman croaking on the floor. He pitched forward, feeling faint, stumbling. Several pens in his shirt pocket came falling out onto the pavement. Regaining his steadiness, he saw the girl's hand moving, groping toward him along the seat. She was only a few inches away when her hand fell limp and she stopped gasping.

The following day, under brilliantly blue skies, fifty thousand dollars' worth of glittering El Dorado streaked across the Golden Gate Bridge, heading north. It was the pimp's car and he was behind the wheel, smiling broadly.

The car was bronze-colored with gold trimmings. The interior was resplendent in all-white mink.

Nearing the end of the bridge, he wove the car into the left lane and zoomed up the Waldo Grade, through the rainbow tunnel. On the other side of the tunnel he saw Mount Tamalpais rising in the distance and Sausalito nestled down under the hills to the right. The pimp sped along for several miles and then moved to the right and off the freeway at the Mill Valley-Stinson Beach exit. He passed several roadside restaurants, motels and service stations as the car wound around a curvy road and stopped at a red light in Tam Junction. From there he turned left and proceeded up through the hills toward the coast. His radio was tuned to the bay area soul station, and he seemed more aware of the music than the road until, casually glancing in the rear-view mirror, he noted, to his dismay, a red light flashing about fifty feet behind him. It was a motorcycle cop.

"Muthafukk!" he blurted out to himself. He took his foot off the accelerator and reached down under the seat, where he kept a .38 stashed. Placing the kill gun between his legs, he pulled the car over to the shoulder. The motorcycle cop drove up alongside. The pimp put a hand on his crotch to cover the gun.

"Good day, sir," the officer said, stepping off the motorcycle and approaching the window.

The pimp shifted in his seat, scowling.

"Is this car registered to you?" the officer asked.

The pimp broke up, laughing mockingly. To reply he used his well-practiced white man's voice: "Yes, this is my car. Is that your motorcycle?"

The officer ignored this remark. He said, "May I see your license and registration, please?"

The pimp continued his mimic of a white voice. "You must be new," he said. "Are you aware of who I am?"

The officer, not indicating whether he was or not, simply replied, "I'm afraid I still have to see your license and registration, sir."

"You have good reason to be afraid," the pimp said, smiling wickedly.

Unfazed, the officer explained, "You were speeding on the bridge, sir."

The pimp widened his smile. He did all he could to restrain himself from laughing again. He was so amused, in fact, that he seemed almost to have forgotten about the gun. The cop continued to stare at him, tolerantly waiting for the papers. The pimp reached into his pocket for a wallet. He shuffled through the cards, in no great hurry. Finally he removed a driver's license, wrapped it in a hundred-dollar bill, and held it between his fingers. Without looking, he handed it to the officer.

For one long second the officer did not move.

The pimp turned to demand a response, but just as he did the officer brought up a long-barreled .357 Magnum.

Even before the pimp's eyes could widen, the silenced gun went off. The pimp gagged as the bullet cut through his neck. The officer unloaded the rest of the clip rapid-fire, then turned around, went back to the motorcycle and drove off.

Chapter 12

The night was clear and crisp, with a full orange moon. Harry Calahan, weary from yet another lethargic day on the stakeout squad, drove home along streets lined with decaying Victorian mansions which had long since been sectioned into cubicle apartments. His own apartment house, a rectangular concrete boxlike structure that resembled a motel, did not quite fit the one-time elegance of the neighborhood. Harry, however, had not chosen to live there for esthetics. Rather, he had picked the place for its location: it was less than ten minutes from the police building. Also, the rent was cheap and the apartment came furnished.

He turned the car into the driveway and drove down into a subterranean garage, parking in a space where the pavement was lettered "CALAHAN" in faded white paint. After cutting the lights and locking the car, he walked from the garage to the sidewalk and then turned up a small stairway leading into the building. As he did so, the blinds in the window of a ground-floor apartment rattled. As tired as he was, Harry was unfailingly alert to all such sounds. He craned his neck and spotted an eye leveled at him from between cracked blinds. As was his habit, he reacted by feeling for the Magnum under his jacket.

He opened the door, walked into the vestibule, unlocked an inner door, checked his mailbox, which was empty except for a gas and electric bill, and started for the stairs. Hearing a door squeak open, he swung around quickly. He was about to pull out his gun when he saw a stunning young Oriental girl, black hair spilling over her shoulders, emerge from the doorway. She had on paint-splattered blue jeans and a tattered workshirt which was unbuttoned to the waist. Her skin was impeccably unblemished and her eyes were very large and alluring. She set them on Harry.

"Hi," she said.

Harry yawned and replied, "Hello."

The girl pushed hair from her face and smiled. She wet her lips, then wrinkled her nose, suggesting that she wanted to say something but wasn't sure whether she should.

Harry answered her expression by saying, "Go ahead."

It was all the encouragement the girl needed. She said, "I've been living here for six months now."

"I work a lot," Harry told her.

"So I've noticed."

Harry smiled inscrutably.

"You're the cop who lives upstairs," the girl said.

"What about it?"

She replied with a long and marvelously direct look. "I have a question for you."

"Oh yeh," Harry said, not inviting it.

"What does a girl have to do to go to bed with you?"

After a short beat of silence, Harry suggested; "Knock on my door."

He continued up the steps.

Without bothering to turn on the lights, Harry walked through the living room and into the kitchen and opened the refrigerator, which he found empty except for a jar of grape jam, a few cans of beer, a bottle of mustard and a greasy paper bag from Joe's diner on Fillmore Street. He removed the bag, along with a can of beer, and headed back into the living room. He sat in a flimsy Danish modern chair. As his eyes became accustomed to the darkness, he looked around and found the room unkempt, with dirty underwear strewn about everywhere and detective magazines piling up in dusty corners. His gaze was indifferent until it fixed on a photograph of himself with a woman. Both he and the woman were laughing. The picture had been snapped just as they were in the midst of cutting a slice of wedding cake. His eyes focused on the woman and grew abstracted. The photo was full of so many memories.

Her name was Bernice. Harry had been married to her for less than a year. In the beginning it had been good between them. She was a clerk in the Department of Motor Vehicles when they met. Harry had just finished his training in the police academy. He was young and eager to start his career as a cop and had neglected to have his driver's license renewed. It was not until the date of expiration, at five minutes to five o'clock, that he found the time to make it to the Department of Motor Vehicles. Bernice stayed a few minutes overtime to save him the inconvenience of coming back the next morning, and afterwards, to show his appreciation, he took her to dinner at Fisherman's Wharf. From there they went to a movie and then back to Bernice's apartment in the Richmond district.

She was new to San Francisco, having moved out not long before from Boston. On her coffee table was a stack of *Cosmopolitan* magazines. She served wine to Harry. She told him that in Boston she had gone to college for three years, until the summer of her junior year, the previous summer, when she had come to San Francisco to visit a girl friend. She liked California so much she decided not to go back East. However, she mentioned several times that she had not yet met any men in whom she was really interested. But she loved San Francisco anyway, she insisted. She chattered on and on, refilling Harry's wine glass numerous times. He became a little drunk.

Bernice was a brunette with a svelte body. Her father was an admiral and she expressed a preference for men in uniform. Growing a bit drunk herself, she told Harry he was the first cop she'd ever met and that she liked him quite a lot. She also liked his high cheekbones, she said, and remarked that she thought the mole over his lip was cute.

They made love.

The following morning they stopped to get a marriage license and then Harry drove her to work at the Department of Motor Vehicles. Three days later they took their case to a Justice of the Peace in Marin County and spent a one-night honeymoon in a motel at Stinson Beach. The romance did not last for long after that. Harry decided he liked being a cop better than a husband. Six months later, they separated.

Harry shook his head sadly, turning away from the photograph. He removed a cold hamburger from the paper bag and popped open the beer can, taking several long swigs. Then, though most people would have found it about as appetizing as cardboard. He wolfed down the entire hamburger in six bites. Finishing, he licked his lips and muttered to himself, "Goddamn thing'll probably kill me." He drained the last of the beer from the can and then was interrupted from any further conversation with himself by a hesitant knocking at the door.

He allowed the sound to pass and went to the refrigerator for another can of beer.

The knocking came a second time, a bit more persistently. With the beer in his hand, Harry walked over and opened the door.

There stood the Oriental girl, wearing an old raincoat, her gorgeous eyes glazed. Her bare legs, showing through a slit in the coat, suggested the possibility that she might be wearing nothing underneath.

"Well," Harry said. "Well."

"Hi." The girl smiled with puckered cheeks.

"Hello." Harry heavily accented the last syllable of the word.

"You always live in the dark?" The girl raised her eyebrows.

"Yeh." Harry grinned. "You meet a better class of people in the dark."

"May I come in?"

Harry extended his arm graciously and the girl stepped inside.

"Beer?" Harry asked her.

"Please." The girl had much presence. She was tall, thin and composed.

"I don't have any clean glasses," Harry said, but not as an apology.

"Cool," the girl replied. "I'll drink it from the can." She walked to the couch and sat down in the dark, pulling her long legs up with her. Harry brought her the beer and sat down next to her.

He took a swig. She did likewise.

"Don't waste any time, do you?" he asked casually.

The girl sent a playful message through her eyes, indicating that she didn't understand what he meant. Harry smiled, then winked, indicating that he thought she was okay. For a moment, neither of them said anything.

Finally the girl, winking too, tried: "Well . . . I knocked."

"Yeh, so you did."

Holding his eyes with hers, she began to slowly unzip the raincoat. Harry took one final, generous swig to finish off the beer, then, just as he put the can down on the floor, the telephone, which rested on an end table, began ringing.

The girl continued to unzip her coat. Harry clicked on a light and reached for the phone.

"Yeh," he said into the receiver.

"Calahan! That you?" It was Briggs. The gruffness in the voice was unmistakable.

The girl fumbled for a cigarette, abandoning the zipper midway. She blinked to show disappointment.

"What is it, Briggs?"

"You alone?"

"No," Harry said, sizing up the girl's legs. "As a matter of fact, I'm in the midst of entertaining a very attractive young lady friend of Oriental descent."

"Well, get your pants back on, Calahan. And get your ass down to the morgue on the double."

"The morgue! What the hell for?"

"You'll find out when you get here, Calahan. Now get moving."

"I'm not Homicide, Briggs, remember? I'm a stakeout man now. See you in the morning, and don't bother me till then."

"Look, Calahan!" Briggs did all he could to hold himself on the edge of civility "Not that it offers me any pleasure to relate this to you, but you and your partner Smith are back on Homicide. *Temporarily,* if I have anything to do with it."

Harry grinned from one ear to the other. "Got one too hot to handle, Briggs?"

"It wasn't my decision, Calahan. You better be sure of that." Briggs hung up.

As Harry put down the receiver he glanced again at the girl's legs, sighed appreciatively, got up, put on his coat, and headed for the door.

"Hey!" the girl demanded. "What happens to me?"

Harry turned, his hand on the doorknob. "What did you want to happen to you?"

"Why, you son of a bitch!" The girl was somewhere between being infuriated and aroused.

Harry was totally amused. Grinning, he said, "Now, the way I see it, you can be stupid or you can be smart."

The girl looked at him, uncertain which one to choose.

But Harry did not wait for her reply. "Keep it warm. I'll be back," he said, and slammed the door.

Chapter 13

Harry passed an all-night newsstand on the corner outside the police building. The short, cigar-chomping newsdealer brightened.

"Hello, Harry," he called.

Harry smiled. "How's retirement, Eddie?" The man was one of his luckier ex-partners.

"It's fine, Harry. As long as the ponies are winning."

Harry grinned, turned and headed into the building. He took the elevator to the basement and proceeded down a long corridor lined on both sides with doors. Passing a double door, he checked himself, heeled around, then backtracked a few steps to a second set of doors, where a uniformed cop stood guard. The cop gave Harry a thumbs-up gesture, which he ignored as he went through the doors.

The room he entered was harshly illuminated with fluorescent lights. Along the walls was a series of chrome refrigerator doors. Set in the middle of the room were two rows of twelve tables each. A corpse covered by a green plastic sheet lay on each table. Only the feet were visible, with an identification tag on each right large toe. Lieutenant Briggs and Captain Paul Avery waited near one of the tables, squinting under the fierce lights.

Avery was a florid-looking man, an old-style cop who had come up the hard way through the ranks. They both straightened when they saw Harry approaching. Avery was no more fond of him than Briggs was, though—unlike Briggs—he recognized that there were times when Dirty Harry's talents could just not be ignored.

"This is a little dramatic, isn't it, Briggs? Not usually your style," Harry remarked, nodding to the two dozen corpses.

"It's meant to be dramatic, Calahan," Briggs growled.

Avery, aware of the intense friction between the two men, intervened by allowing, "Calahan, this thing might be bigger than even we think it is."

"Meaning?" Harry curled his bushy eyebrows.

"Meaning this," Avery replied, heading down the row of bodies, lifting certain toe tags. "Hijacking and gambling—trucking—waterfront—garbage, citywide—gambling—narcotics and prostitution—gambling and waterfront—narcotics and gambling—trucking and narcotics—prostitution—". Then suddenly he stopped midway down the line, waved his hand over all the bodies and turned to face Harry. "This, whether you know it or not, Calahan, is the cream in the bottle. It's a good bet there's somebody out there who's trying to put the courts out of business."

"So far you haven't said anything wrong," Harry granted. "Except you still haven't told me anything I wouldn't know just from reading the papers."

Avery shot him a slightly less than tolerant look and called to a lab technician across the room. "Wheel over those other two," he said.

The technician slid out two more tables. Avery walked over to one and lifted a tag on a big black toe. "This," he said, "just came in a few hours ago. It looks like somebody wants it all. This guy was just a small-time pimp." And then, indicating the other body, "That's one of his girls."

Harry lifted the sheet on the woman and wondered aloud, "What happened to her?"

"A cab driver brought her in last night. Before her friend here got plugged himself," Avery indicated the pimp, "he poured a bottle of drain opener down her throat."

"Drain opener?" Harry marveled. "Well, that does show a certain sense of style, now, doesn't it?"

"You're all heart, Calahan," Briggs interrupted. His upper lip twitched and his eyes swelled with venom. He did all he could to contain himself. It had been Avery's decision to call in Harry Calahan. Left alone to his own devices, Briggs would have left him assigned permanently to stakeout.

Harry, acutely aware of Briggs's enmity, looked at Avery, pointing to the lieutenant with his thumb. "Is he going to be looking over my shoulder every time I turn around? Because if he is, you can figure it's going to take me twice as long to finish the job."

Avery, annoyed by the question, nonetheless resolved it by declaring, "You work *with* Briggs on this one, Calahan. *With!* Do I make myself clear? But if you lean out of line—just once—so help me, I'll flop you lower than whaleshit."

"While we're on the subject of whaleshit," Harry said, stroking his chin, "I'd like to ask Briggs here what he's come up with so far?"

"I don't have to stand here and take that kind of abuse," Briggs erupted.

"I don't believe that answers my question," Harry persisted.

"For your information, nobody in my department is sitting on their ass, Calahan!"

"I don't believe that answers it either."

"Enough!" Avery insisted. He sighed and removed a small electronic telephone-answering device from his breast pocket. He held it up, speaking with a pained expression on his face. "Calahan, you see this thing? The chief! He calls me all the time on this one—even in the can. I haven't been out of my shoes in days and still we have no witnesses. Not a single one! Now, I want this case cracked and I don't want any goddamn nonsense. Whoever our man is, he's no amateur. So you got your work cut out. To show you how good he is—in every one of these cases an officer's been right there at the scene of the crime, but as yet none of them—not a single one—has seen a damn thing."

"Who reported this last hit?" Harry wanted to know, flicking the identification tag on the pimp's toe.

"A patrolman. Sweet, I think his name was. Is that right, Briggs?"

Briggs nodded affirmatively.

"He's a good man," Harry noted. "A good man." Then

he turned to Briggs and said, "I'll start with all the ballistics reports in the morning, first thing."

"We ran all the slugs through ballistics already," Briggs told him. "We're never going to see those guns. It was too professional. You're wasting your time."

Harry replied to Briggs for Avery's benefit, saying, "That's all right, Briggs, if you don't mind I'll run the slugs through again. I'm sort of an old-fashioned detective."

Briggs glared at him.

"Oh yeh, and one other thing, Briggs. I may have already told you this, but it's worth repeating: a smart man knows his limitations."

When Harry returned to his apartment it was almost midnight. He was extremely weary—and a little bit on edge. Without turning on any lights, he pulled off his jacket, tie and shirt and threw them on the couch. Half undressed, he started for the refrigerator but then stopped suddenly when he heard something stirring in the bedroom. He drew his gun, swung around and kicked the bedroom door open—all in one continuous movement.

There was utter silence as he stood in the doorway, gun poised.

When his eyes adjusted to the darkness, he found, to his pleasure and amusement, a guest in the bed waiting for him. She was the Oriental girl, half under the sheets. She looked up seductively as he walked slowly to the foot of the bed.

"Warm enough?" she asked.

Harry grinned. It certainly was.

"You're going to be my first cop." She smiled expectantly.

Chapter 14

Harry Calahan awoke earlier than usual the following morning, dressed, shaved, and, leaving the Oriental girl still asleep in his bed, headed to the police building. He phoned ahead so that Early Smith and a technician, Walter Smathers, would be waiting for him in the ballistics lab.

"It's all set up for you, Harry. That microscope over there," Walter told him when he walked in. He and Early were having coffee.

Harry took a seat at the microscope. He rubbed his palms together eagerly and then put his eye to work. He carefully studied the grooves and striations on two bullets, and then did likewise with a third bullet. All the bullets matched almost perfectly, back to back. It was obvious that they had been fired from the same pistol. Grimacing, Harry backed away from the microscope and swiveled his chair around to face Early and Walter. They were standing by a window. Brilliant morning sunshine flooded the room, causing Harry to blink several times to clear his vision.

"What do the others look like?" he wanted to know.

Walter scratched his neck. "The gun was a .357 Magnum," he said. "These are the only three bullets we have, though. The others are all too deformed to do us any good—hollow points—fired point blank, you know."

Harry nodded.

Walter added, "Actually we were lucky to get that last bullet. I found it in the mink carpeting."

Harry turned back to the microscope and took another look. He drew his lips together tightly and tapped on the table. "Well," he said, "they're very sharply grooved from rifling. I'd say the gun's got a target-grade barrel."

"Probably right," Walter confirmed.

"Doesn't do much, but narrows it down some, I guess," Harry sighed.

"Yeh." Walter laughed through his nose. "Like narrows it down to you and maybe a thousand other guys who do serious target shooting, not to mention, say, a couple of hundred cops or so."

Harry lifted his eyes from the microscope on the word *cops*.

"Maybe it is a cop!" Early blurted out playfully. He tried laughing, though neither Harry nor Walter found the remark particularly funny. "Maybe it's Harry! After all, nobody hates hoodlums as much as he does!"

Walter sputtered a reluctant laugh. Harry reacted by bolting Early with unamused eyes.

"Well, you know," Early explained, "I'm only trying to be funny."

"Don't try so hard," Harry told him.

Early shrugged defenselessly.

"Okay, Walter," Harry said, "let's have a look at the pimp's car."

The three men walked to the garage, where the Eldorado sat in a flood of natural light streaming down from a row of windows near the ceiling. A series of taut wires marked the trajectories of the bullets, extending from the driver's seat outward to a point where they all came together. The car took on the appearance of a rare animal that had been harpooned. Farther away and off to one corner of the garage, Harry saw several technicians performing a similar operation on Carmine Ricca's limousine.

"Whoever it is," Walter said, pondering the El Dorado, "he enjoys it. The pimp was dead with the first shot. The others were only for good measure. The killer unloaded a whole clip in him. You can see—most of the slugs were right on top of one another."

Harry blew out a mouthful of smoke.

"One big mothering hole," was the way Early saw it.

Walter said, "The mortician couldn't even put the face back together."

Early shook his head sadly.

"Everybody has to pay something," was Harry's comment.

Walter situated himself a few feet from the door of the car, near the driver's window. "The killer had to be this close," he commented, aiming a finger into the car. "Point-blank range." He touched the point where all the wires met.

"Christ!" Early shut his eyes.

"What about the license?" Harry asked.

"There was a hundred-dollar bill wrapped around it," Walter said.

"Where was it held?"

Walter pointed to the spot. "Right about here, from what we figure."

"Showing it to a traffic cop?" Harry wondered aloud.

"Yeh," Walter said. "That's what it looks like to us. From everything we have, Harry, it figures out to be somebody impersonating a police officer. Same as the job they did on Ricca. It's been done before. And if you don't mind me saying so, Harry, these guys are all pros. The pimp—"

"Guys?"

"Just a guess. Could be there's only one. But as I was saying, the pimp had a .38 on the seat between his legs. He never even had a chance to use it. That's how professional this job was. When we found him, the pimp didn't even have his finger on the trigger. So, like with Carmine Ricca, whoever the killer was it figures he had to be somebody the victims would never recognize."

"Or never suspect," Harry added thoughtfully.

Later in the morning Briggs summoned Early and Harry, along with several other detectives, to the projection room. Briggs began the session by showing mug shots and photos of all the men so far assassinated. Each slide which flashed on the screen bore a large grease-penciled X across the face. One by one, Briggs read off the names, detailing each with thumbnail biographies. When he finished he inserted another tray of slides into the projector and lit a cigar.

The first slide in the new tray did not have an X across it. It was a mug shot of a stubby bull-like man, balding and coarse-featured. The man's face was stiff and arrogant. Harry took a drag off his cigarette and sat up, sneering at the screen.

"Lou Guzman," Briggs said, identifying the mug. "Ex-meat lugger with a first-grade education—started working for the old bosses as a hitter. He controls narcotics statewide these days—dabbles in prostitution—has big friends everywhere."

Briggs stopped for a brief moment to take in the cluster of detectives staring intently at Guzman. "Casale and Di-Gorgio—he's all yours."

In the darkened room Jim Casale, a bland middle-aged workhorse of a detective, drew an anxious breath. Sal Di-Gorgio, the weary-looking man sitting beside Casale—he had a reputation as one of the better detectives on the squad—scratched his ear and grimaced painfully. Neither man said anything.

A second slide flashed on the screen. It was a group photograph of a half dozen tough, burly men. They were all dressed in extravagantly colored shirts, and smiling broadly. The photo had been taken in an elegant tropical setting, which could have conceivably been either Palm Springs or Palm Beach, though it was not possible to determine which one. The background appeared to be a golf course. Five of the men stood off to one side of the picture, watching the sixth man, who on close inspection Harry recognized as the late Carmine Ricca, receive a tournament trophy. A red circle was drawn in grease pencil around one of the five men, the fattest. Harry squinted to see who it was.

"Okay, Calahan," Briggs announced, "this one is for your special talents."

Harry was still unable to recognize the face. The man was grinning with all the warmth of a bulldozer. He wore dark glasses.

"Frank Imperial," Briggs continued. "Two hundred and eighty-two pounds—indicted for murder twenty-three times—no convictions. Complains a lot about his health now—suffers from ulcers and migraine headaches—he's dangerously violent. He was once Ricca's principal assassin. If you mix with him, he won't back off. He's all yours, Calahan."

"You're all heart, Briggs," Harry called out. "But I don't think—"

"I don't care what you think."

"—he has anything to do with these hits."

"Calahan," Briggs boomed, "I said I want you on him! Period!"

Another slide flashed on the screen but before Briggs could identify it, Harry spoke up again. He said: "Imperial is a snake, Briggs. I'd burn him for stepping on a crack in the sidewalk if I could. But these hits are not his style. Not the cars, anyway. Too direct."

Every detective in the room, including Early, sank low in his seat. All eyes shifted to Briggs. If the two most stubborn men in the entire department had to be singled out, they would almost certainly be Calahan and Briggs—and here they were locking horns for all to see.

"Calahan," Briggs shouted, "your orders are to keep your nose pressed up against Imperial's ass until I get a warrant from the D.A.'s office to bring him in! Now if you don't like the assignment, maybe it's time you retired. So take your choice. I want this animal Imperial! I'm going to be the first one to get a conviction on the bastard!"

All heads turned to Harry, who did not appear to be disturbed in the least by the lieutenant's rising tone of voice.

"A conviction?" he said, his voice full of undisguised contempt. "Be serious, Briggs. The way I figure, Imperial's more likely to be the next *victim*. Come on, what are you really asking for?"

"I'm not ASKING anything, Calahan. I'm TELLING. For the last goddamn time, your orders are to keep your nose on Imperial's ass!"

Chapter 15

Frank Imperial operated out of a dingy-looking warehouse in the Embarcadero. It was a one-story rectangular building, sorely in need of a fresh coat of paint. A faded sign over the door read: Imperial's Imported Foods Company. Importing pasta and bottled tomato sauce from Italy was Frank Imperial's claim to being a legitimate businessman.

Harry Calahan and Early Smith established their stakeout position across the street from the warehouse in a vacant room above a boarded-up Italian restaurant.

Harry was settled against a bare wall with the *Examiner* as Early sat on a wooden chair near the window, peeking through a crack in the boards. For the first hour there was no movement in or out of the warehouse. When Harry finished the paper he took a short nap. He woke up twenty minutes later, yawning. He lit a cigarette and amused himself by blowing smoke circles. Then he got up and began pacing around the room. He was very restless.

"This is bullshit," he said.

Early looked up at him noncommittally, then glanced at his watch. It was nine o'clock. The night was dark and the only light came from a single streetlamp out front.

Harry walked to the window to have a look. Propped up next to the wall near the window were several Invicta shotguns and a .308 Norma Magnum rifle with scoped sight. Looking out, Harry saw a man emerge from the warehouse and close the door quickly behind himself. He watched as the man took a few steps out into the street, glancing up and down in both directions before retreating back inside. It appeared to be nothing but a routine maneuver.

"At least we know they're in there," Early remarked.

Harry grunted. He went back to slouch against the wall and closed his eyes again. Several minutes later he snapped awake to the sound of something scurrying under the floorboards.

"Rats," Early explained, watching his partner stir.

"How can a man sleep with rats under his bed?" Harry growled bitterly. "What's happening out there?"

"Nothing," Early said. "Not a thing."

"Figures. Briggs is full of shit."

Early, too diplomatic to comment on this observation, noted expansively, "You know, I once knew an old guy who kept pigs under his bed."

Harry looked at him as if to say, "So what?" But instead he kept his mouth shut.

"Strange fella," Early continued.

"What kind of pigs? The eating kind?" Harry was so bored he was even ready to submit to small talk.

His question brought a laugh from Early. "The eating kind! Is that all you ever think about? Your stomach?"

"What's it to you, man?"

"Just kidding, Harry, that's all."

Harry paused and then decided to ask: "Why did the guy keep pigs under his bed?"

"Well, I don't know how much you know about pigs, but—"

"Plenty."

"Well, it's easy enough to sell a pig, but what's not so easy is to know when to sell it."

"Smith, is this going to be another one of your 'back home in Georgia' stories?"

Early smiled, unjarred by the insult. He continued, "Well, this old boy knew the pigs were big enough to make bacon when they started raising the bed under him, scratching their backs. When he couldn't sleep he knew the pigs were done."

"Ha, ha," Harry said, obviously not amused.

"What's eating you?" Early finally asked.

Without answering Harry got up and put on his jacket. At the door he said, "I'll be back."

"Hey, wait a minute. We're supposed to—where you going?"

The door slammed shut.

When he rang the doorbell Harry Calahan heard a television playing inside the apartment. Footsteps came toward the door and a woman's voice asked, "Who is it?"

"It's me, Harry."

"Harry!" The door swung open. The woman was so delighted to see him that she almost giggled with pleasure.

"Hi, Carol," he said somberly.

"Anything the matter?" she wondered. "Come in. Would you like a beer or something?"

"No thanks." Harry said, stepping in. He did not sit down. "I have to find Charlie, Carol. Where do I start looking?"

The question disappointed and frightened her at the same time. Finally she said, "Well . . . I—don't know. Can't you stay awhile? Is it urgent?"

He hesitated, not answering either of her questions.

"What is it, Harry?" she insisted.

"I have to talk to him, that's all."

"Did he . . . uh . . . has he . . . uh . . . uh . . ." She was unable to form the question.

"Carol, please. I don't have much time. Where do I start looking?"

"Oh, Harry!" She burst into tears and fell into his arms. He consoled her for a moment and then pushed her off gently, holding on to her shoulders.

"It may be nothing," he assured her.

Through her sobbing she managed, "He doesn't know I know this, but that tramp he's been running around with works as a, uh, you know, at that topless and bottomless place on the corner of Broadway and Columbus. But I don't know where he lives. Nob Hill somewhere. Maybe she does."

"What's her name?"

"I don't know."

"Carol." He didn't believe her. "There's not much time."

"Harry, tell me, you must. What did he do?"

"What's her name, Carol?"

"She goes by the name of Lotta Bliss."

The man standing out front was barking, "See it with your own eyes! Totally nude college coeds! Erotic love dances! Live sexual acts on stage!"

Harry shoved by him and walked inside. A middle-aged balding man approached him, asking if he'd like a table up front.

"Police," Harry replied, flashing the badge.

All color drained from the man's face. He turned around quickly to see what was happening on the stage, where two women were making love to one another on a satin-covered bed. The audience was cheering them on with catcalls.

The man turned back to Harry with nervous eyes.

"Is one of them named Lotta Bliss?"

The man hesitated. Then he said, "The blond."

"Tell her I want to talk to her."

"She'll be off in a few minutes, officer."

"Now!"

"Yes, sir." The man reluctantly lumbered to the edge of the stage. The women were in the midst of fondling each other's breasts. He stood on his toes and whispered something to the blond. Her partner, a redheaded black woman, shot him a fierce glance. The man shrugged, climbed to the stage and apologized. "Ladies and gentlemen, there will be a short interruption in the show. The young ladies will be back in a few minutes."

The audience booed wildly. The women stepped off the stage and into robes.

Harry waited off to the side for the blond. She was a young girl, in her early twenties, with blue eyes. Though her face showed promise, Harry decided that she looked better in the robe than she did on the stage.

"What's this all about, copper?" she demanded. "I'm clean."

"Where's Charlie McCoy?" Harry raised one eye and lowered a lid over the other.

The blond caressed her knuckles. "I don't know anybody by that name," she said.

"Get your clothes on. You're coming down to the station with me."

The blond stiffened. "I ain't done nothin' wrong!"

Harry smirked and tipped his head toward the empty stage.

The blond pursed her lips. "The law, in case you don't know it, copper, says I got a right to take my clothes off up there."

"I got another law in mind," Harry told her. "One that says that when two people do it, one's got to be a man and the other's got to be a woman."

The blond shriveled.

"Now if you want to save yourself some trouble, lady, tell me where I can find Charlie McCoy. And this is the last time I'm asking."

"I haven't seen him in three weeks."

"Where does he live?"

"I don't remember."

"Get dressed." He took her arm.

She jerked away. "Okay, copper, you win."

"Let's have it."

"The last I heard of him," she said, "he had a place on Nob Hill. I'm not sure of the address. It's on Powell, the corner of Chestnut. Right-hand side, facing north. That's all I know. And if you happen to find him, copper, tell him I haven't forgot about the five hundred bucks he owes me."

Harry said, "Tell him yourself," turned around and walked out.

Harry found Charlie McCoy's name on the mailbox in the small apartment building. Apartment 4-F. The elevator was out of order, so he stalked up the steps, two at a time. He knocked on the door several times, but there was no answer.

He tried the door next to it. A middle-aged woman answered, her hair in curlers.

"I'm looking for Charlie McCoy," Harry told her. "When's the last time you saw him?"

."I don't know anybody by that name," the woman said, starting to shut the door in Harry's face. He stopped it with his foot.

"He's your neighbor in 4-F," Harry said.

"You mean the policeman?"

"Yeh."

She eyed Harry suspiciously, demanding, "Who are you?"

"A friend."

"Well, if he's a friend of yours you ought to have him committed to a mental hospital."

"What do you mean by that?"

"My husband went over to ask him to turn his television down the other night, because we couldn't sleep. When he came to the door he had a gun in his hand. My husband almost had a heart attack on the spot. Your friend, whatever his name is, pointed the gun between my husband's eyes and said the only reason he wasn't going to pull the trigger then and there was because he didn't have a silencer on the gun. He accused my husband of working for the Mafia. The man is crazy."

Chapter 16

It was not until twenty minutes after eleven o'clock that Harry arrived back at the Imperial stakeout. He found Early Smith in a near frenzy.

"Jesus, Harry, where've you been?"

"Out to lunch." Harry walked directly to the window. "Any action while I was gone?"

"An awful lot of checking and peeking, peeking and checking. Jesus, Harry, if Briggs knew what you—"

"Fuck Briggs," Harry yawned.

"You sure do like to have things your own way," Early said, shaking his head.

"That's because my way is right," Harry explained. He motioned for Early to get off the chair. "Take a rest."

Just as Early got up, suddenly, from across the street, came the sound of a steel garage door rumbling open.

"Sounds like the fun's just about to start," Harry remarked. Early joined him at the window and they watched as two men emerged from the garage door, looking up and down the street. The men gave a signal and out roared three cars—two Buicks and a Cadillac.

"Jesus." Early did a double take.

"All right," Harry said. "Let's go."

They ran down the back steps and outside to the car, which Harry had parked behind the building. They leaped in, Early taking the wheel.

"Lights?" he asked Harry.

"Not yet," Harry figured. "Wait till we get going."

Early wheeled the car out of the alley and made it to the street just in time to catch a glimpse of the second Buick disappearing around the corner. Early put the lights on and stepped on the gas. He finally caught the Imperial caravan several blocks farther on. The three cars turned onto a main street, passed a lot of traffic and neon, and continued to a freeway entrance. Early tagged at a safe distance, neither too close to be detected nor too far to be left behind. However, in a few miles the freeway abruptly split off into a Y, and the three cars separated. The lead car, a Buick, turned off toward the Bay Bridge and Oakland, while the other two headed for the Golden Gate Bridge.

"Five zero six ten four," Early said into the radio. "They're splitting up on us." He then swung around to Harry, asking, "Which way?"

"Follow the two," Harry told him.

"Five zero six ten four," Early reported into the radio. "We're taking the Golden Gate turnoff."

"Roger," a voice in the radio crackled.

They tailed the two cars over the Golden Gate Bridge and started up the Waldo Grade into Marin County. At the last moment the Cadillac veered right and got off at a Sausalito exit. The Buick remained on the freeway.

"Which way now?" Early wanted to know.

"Always follow the money," Harry said.

Early cut hard to the right and drove down the exit ramp. For a moment he lost the Cadillac on the winding roads. He increased speed, came around a curve, and found the Cadillac stopped by the side of the road. He was forced to drive on by.

"Jesus," Early muttered, then made a clucking sound with his mouth.

Harry angrily slammed his hand into the dashboard. "He's on to us," he fumed. Then he bit his lip and re-solved, "Nothing we can do about it." Watching in the rear-view mirror, he saw the Cadillac back up, turn around, and head back toward the freeway.

"Pull over!" he ordered Early. "Let me drive."

Early pulled off the road and they changed places. Harry whipped the car up a driveway, backed out, and, squealing rubber, made his way back up to the Cadillac's tail, hanging in at no more than a car's length from the bumper.

"What are you trying to do, Harry?" Early nervously protested. "Imperial doesn't know we're cops. He may panic and—"

Harry, clenching the steering wheel, cut him off, arguing, "Imperial! I hope he does panic, that bastard. I'll get him for twenty-three other murders. And if he doesn't panic, I might be right about something that's been nagging me. I hope I'm not."

"What?" Early popped straight up. "Christ, Harry, I don't want to be winning bets for anybody."

"You worry too much," Harry told him.

The Cadillac picked up speed and screeched back onto the freeway, heading south to San Francisco. The driver swung into the slow lane, extending a hand out the window, indicating that he wanted Harry to pass.

"It may be a trap," Early warned anxiously.

If it were, Harry didn't care. He put his .44 Magnum between his legs and signaled for Early to ready the shotgun.

Early closed his eyes for a very brief moment of prayer, then cocked the gun.

Harry pulled the car into the middle lane, moving up toward the Cadillac. As he approached he could see Frank Imperial and four hitters in the car, their faces as dark as the night.

"Hey, go a little faster," Early pleaded urgently. "I'm the one who's on their side."

"Roll down your window," Harry told him.

"What!"

"You heard me."

"You're crazy, Harry."

"Just do what I say, and don't worry about it. Have I ever been wrong?"

"Jesus Christ," Early said, rolling up his eyes and rolling down the window. "I really don't know why the hell I'm doing this."

Harry pulled the car up directly alongside the Cadillac, traveling at fifty miles per hour, and shouted at the top of his voice: "Hey, I need some help!"

"Wha?" The driver, a gruff-looking unshaven man, appeared startled.

"I'm lost," Harry shouted. "I missed the exit to San Quentin. I'm wondering whether you fellas might know where it is?"

The driver snarled, "It's back there." He motioned over his shoulder with a thumb. "What's a matter? Can't you see right or something?"

"Oh, I can see fine," Harry shot back. "I just wanted to see if you fellas knew where it was—because it won't be long before you'll all be moving there!"

Saying that, Harry stepped on the accelerator and sped ahead of the Cadillac. Early let out a sigh of relief, nearly laughing out of pure nervousness.

Harry said, "Someday I'm going to get those sons of bitches, if it's the last thing I do."

Early looked at him, startled. He opened his mouth, but no words came out.

"Bastards," Harry said.

Finally, collecting himself, Early found his voice. "You always do things your own way, Harry."

"You got it."

"No wonder Briggs is always on your ass."

Harry holstered his gun as he brought the car onto the bridge. With a grin, he observed, "You take your life in your hands when you do things someone else's way."

"Well, I just did it your way!" Early reminded him.

"That's because I'm better." Harry smiled.

Chapter 17

Sal DiGorgio stood at the window of a completely dark and empty apartment on Telegraph Hill, adjusting a pair of mounted high-powered binoculars. His partner, Jim Casale, rested on a folding chair nearby, reading a newspaper as best he could by making the most of the available sunlight. Both men, having been in the apartment for almost eighteen hours straight, were tired and edgy. The floor around them was littered with used paper coffee cups. Standing against the wall were two .308 Norma Magnum rifles with telescopic sights.

DiGorgio focused the binoculars on a bodyguard lounging at the entrance to a luxury apartment building across the street. He studied the man for a moment, then lifted the binoculars for a look at the penthouse apartment in the building, where drapes in all but a few of the windows were drawn. Briefly, he saw a silhouette moving from one room to another.

"Son of a bitch," DiGorgio sighed, turning from the binoculars to look Casale full in the eye. "Guzman hasn't gone out once all day!"

Casale crumpled the newspaper in his lap and shook his head exasperatedly.

It was a spectacular bathroom full of baroque trimmings, marble and gold touches, more ostentatious than tasteful, but nonetheless expensive. Lou Guzman liked almost anything that was expensive. He stood, sunk in the mink carpet of the bathroom, examining his mug in the mirror. He had installed special soft lighting which made him look younger, but even so there was just so much a man could do to lessen the toll of his accumulating years. And Guzman, no two ways about it, was getting old.

He ran a hand over his few remaining strands of hair and grew irritated, swearing under his breath. He then reached into the medicine cabinet, removed a bottle of cologne and splashed some on his face. Turning at a slight angle to highlight what he felt was his better side, he glanced back into the mirror, trying to smile. Although the mirror held a face burdened by a set of small flat eyes, flabby cheeks, an oversized mouth and a crooked nose—indeed, not much to smile over—Guzman stiffened his shoulders, arched up proudly and beamed at himself from ear to ear. He picked his chin up a few degrees to improve the view. He brushed his teeth, shut off the lights and left the room.

He walked down a hallway toward an ornate and enormous bedroom, where a nude couple waited for him, cavorting on a king-size water bed. The girl was in her early twenties, perhaps even younger. By even the most discriminating standards she looked spectacular—long shiny blond hair, a stately face, enormous blue eyes, long perfectly shaped legs and a perfect centerfold figure. The boy, also in his late teens or early twenties, could have almost been her male twin—right down to the flowing blond hair. She was propped against a mass of fur pillows, sniffing cocaine from a tiny gold spoon as he stroked her leg enticingly, giggling. After loading up each nostril, she caused the water bed to shimmer like a bowl of jelly, too stoned to realize what she was doing.

"Mmmmm," she said dreamily.

"Be careful! Don't spill it! He'll kill us—that's his prime stuff," the boy said in a loud whisper, grabbing the cocaine.

"Fuck him," the girl replied, refusing to be hassled. She was not aware that Guzman had entered the room and was at that moment standing over the bed about to undo the buckle on his belt.

"Hey!" he growled. "I ever hear you say that again, broad, and it's your ass!"

The girl blinked several times and sputtered out a half-hearted apology.

"That stuff costs nine hundred an ounce," Guzman reminded her. "You better not spill it. If you do, I'll—"

"Oh come on, Lou," the girl smirked. "Don't be so uptight."

Guzman removed his hand from his belt and waved a fist. "Nobody says that to me!" he said furiously. "Nobody! Don't you ever say that to me again!"

The girl was startled by his sudden temper, and quickly apologized. "I'm sorry, I won't."

Breathing heavily, Guzman proceeded to undress until his misshaped body was totally nude. He glanced down at himself self-consciously, then went to sit on the edge of the bed.

The girl moved up and winked at him as he sunk in.

Lou Guzman snickered at her.

She winked at him again.

This time he stared her straight in the eye.

She took this as a cue to start the action. Seductively, rolling her tongue over her upper lip, she slithered up to him. The boy did likewise, extending the cocaine to Guzman.

Guzman shot his hand up to refuse it and gave the boy a leery look. "Don't be silly," he said, an edge of scorn to his voice. Like so many other narcotics czars, Lou Guzman never touched the stuff. Strangely enough, his aversion to the drug was as much a matter of principle as taste. The boy shrugged and took another hit for himself. The girl leaned over to have her nose filled, too.

After savoring a couple of hits, she swayed forward and put her fingers to work mixing gentle patterns on Lou Guzman's chest. Guzman's body, once firm and muscled, had long ago gone to fat. He immediately closed his eyes and began to moan and writhe under her touch. In a moment or so he opened his eyes again and motioned to the boy by nodding his head. The boy moved up, flirtatiously contacting Guzman's hairy body. His hand joined the girl's on Guzman's chest.

Guzman, annoyed by a lamp on a bedside table, suddenly commanded, "Turn off the lights. I can't stand lights."

The boy reached over and flicked off the switch, causing the water bed to tremble for a moment. The room took on an orange hue from a candle burning on the dresser. Guzman stared at the boy, a lascivious leer glinting in his eyes.

The girl sensed something else in Guzman's look. "What's the matter, Lou?" she asked, thinking he was angry.

"I just hope he's clean, that's all," Guzman grunted.

"Don't worry, Lou," the girl assured him. "I checked him out personally while we were waiting for you."

Guzman brought the back of his hand up and was about to swipe her across the face when the boy slithered up, distracting him. Guzman's mouth parted. When the boy touched him on the genitals, he fell back on the bed, vengeance giving way to lust.

In the stakeout apartment across the street, DiGorgio was having trouble keeping his eyes open when he heard the roar of a motorcycle outside and snapped awake. As he focused the binoculars, Casale scrambled for a rifle.

"Hold it," DiGorgio told him, extending a hand upward in caution. "It's nothing. It's just a cop—a legitimate one. I recognize him."

Casale went to the window and had a look for himself. He saw the cop head into the garage of Lou Guzman's apartment building. DiGorgio continued to peer through the glasses at the man.

"Probably just going to the head," he remarked. "Those guys in Traffic sure develop lousy kidneys from riding motorcycles all day."

Casale squinted for a better look at the man. Unable to place the face, he asked, "You sure you know who that is, Sal?"

"Yeh," DiGorgio said, "that's Charlie McCoy."

In the shadows of a huge block of air-conditioning apparatus on the roof of Lou Guzman's building, a motorcycle cop, wearing black gloves, removed two large sweat socks from a pocket in his leather jacket and pulled them over the bottom of his boots. He straightened up, looked around quickly in all directions and then slipped over a gate to a flight of steel stairs. Noiselessly descending the steps, his face obscured in the shadows, he reached a door and produced a set of keys from his pocket. He picked the correct one with the help of the moonlight, and inserted it into the lock.

A husky bodyguard was stationed on the other side of the door, the only vulnerable access to Lou Guzman's penthouse. When he heard the lock rattling, he tensed and drew his gun. As the door began to open slowly, the guard flattened against the wall, hesitating to see whether the intruder was only the janitor. When the door swung all the way open, he saw, to his utter astonishment, a cop standing there holding a handgun. But before the guard could even close his fallen jaw the cop plugged him with three lightning-fast shots. The shots were silenced, sounding like thuds. The bodyguard gasped and fell, clutching himself, to the floor. The cop, without even looking at him, stepped over the body and into a hallway. He came to another door a few feet away, this one open. He proceeded through without any obstruction.

A few steps farther on he reached a third door, the rear entrance to Guzman's penthouse. He again produced a ring of keys, testing several until he found the one that fit the lock. He clutched the doorknob, hesitating for a beat, then turned it, opening the door a crack. There was no response from inside. He tiptoed in.

The vestibule was completely dark except for a dim red hue coming from a colored light bulb overhead. The cop streaked through a fashionably decorated reception area, then turned in to a hallway. He heard a girl's voice giggling and stopped in the doorway of the room from which it came. Looking in, he saw Guzman and his two playmates entwined on the water bed.

Guzman stirred, then broke away from the couple, sensing something wrong. A look of panic inched across his face. He broke into a cold sweat, beads of moisture collecting over his eyebrows and upper lip. Then suddenly the telephone rang, and it thoroughly undid him. He jerked up, causing a wave in the water bed, and reached out to the end table where the phone rested. The boy and girl, very stoned, flinched back, startled by the sudden commotion.

"What's happening?" the boy asked, his drugged voice leaving long spaces between each syllable.

The girl, less curious, went on teasing herself by tossing her long hair back and forth across her face. She closed her eyes for a split instant and then when she opened them, just as Guzman was picking up the telephone, she saw the cop lurking in the doorway behind an outstretched arm in which he held his gun aimed at her. She gasped and broke into an ear-splitting scream.

Guzman dropped the phone and lunged for a high-powered gun in the top drawer of the end table, but he was nowhere near close to getting to it when the cop opened fire. The boy bolted upright, his eyes wide as saucers. The girl's scream rose even a few shrieking notes higher. The rapid-fire tore through the bed and into Guzman. The cop then whipped into the room, crouched, and continued shooting with the silenced revolver. One bullet caved the boy in. The girl lunged up and stumbled to the window, where the bullets finally met her too and blew her through the glass into a fifteen-story plunge. The nude bodies of Guzman and the boy tangled on the bed and dropped over lifelessly. For a brief second the bullets had turned the bed into a series of geysers and then the water came down, splashing the flesh of the two dead men before rolling off onto the white carpeting.

The cop pulled the socks off his boots and ran out.

The bodyguard at the street entrance saw the nude blond hit the pavement, screaming. He wheeled around and darted inside the building, gun drawn, dragging two people out of the elevator and hijacking it up to the penthouse, a finger flat against the button the whole way. After taking a quick look at the bloody scene in the penthouse, he raced back to the elevator.

DiGorgio and Casale heard the shots and the screaming and took off furiously for Guzman's apartment. They found themselves delayed, for a few brief but crucial moments, trying to get through a fast stream of traffic plowing down the street.

In the garage, the restroom door banged open and Charlie McCoy, unaware that anything peculiar was taking place in or around the building, started back to his motorcycle after having washed off his bruised hand. Suddenly, hearing footsteps clobbering down the steel stairs, he swung around and reached for his gun, trotting cautiously toward the fire exit. Crouching in front of a car, he aimed expertly with both hands and waited for the door to open.

When it did, Charlie shouted: "Hold it! Police!"

But then he realized that the man was only Ben Davis, a colleague in Traffic. McCoy inhaled deeply, starting to sigh his relief when Davis drew his gun and plugged him three times. The only sound was the dull thud of silenced slugs puncturing Charlie's heart. When he hit the ground, McCoy was already dead. He took with him to the grave a look of utter surprise on his lifeless face.

Davis was reloading his gun just as Guzman's bodyguard burst through the door, racing to find a car in which to escape the premises before the police arrived. When he saw Davis, in his police uniform, he opened fire, but his shots were wild and they missed the patrolman by a substantial angle. Davis wheeled and fired, unloading the entire fresh clip. The bodyguard slammed against a wall, dead.

Davis stood for a moment, holding the smoking gun in his hand before holstering it. He caught his breath, adjusted his helmet, and mopped his forehead with the sweat socks he absently pulled from his pocket.

A crowd collected swiftly outside around the entrance to the garage. There was a lot of shoving and a great deal of clamor, with everyone asking one another if they knew what was going on. There was much discussion about the fallen nude blond, over whose head Jim Casale placed his sports jacket.

DiGorgio broke through the crowd and into the garage. It startled him when he came up against a man dusting off the sleeve of his patrolman's uniform. He recognized the man as Ben Davis.

"There's been a little trouble here, Sal," Davis said, his voice extremely calm.

DiGorgio was still too shocked to speak.

"They killed a cop," Davis told him.

Chapter 18

Sitting tall behind his desk, with the telephone clutched tightly in one hand, Detective Lieutenant Neil Briggs looked haggard and jittery. The angry, insistent voice at the other end of the line was that of his superior, Captain Paul Avery, who was in the midst of delivering a torrent of furious words to the effect that Harry Calahan had brains "up his ass." Finding no argument there, Briggs kept inserting "Yes, sir . . . yes, sir" into Avery's tirade, but the captain was not placated. He informed Briggs, in no uncertain terms, that he too was incompetent, and that he would be held responsible for any future improprieties on Calahan's part.

"Is that clear, Briggs?" Avery said finally.

"Yes, sir," Briggs replied pleadingly. "It won't happen again. I give you my word."

"One other thing, Briggs. I don't want any of this to get out to the press. Because if it does, you're—"

"It won't, sir. You have my word." Briggs cut him short, hoping to keep the threatened consequences ambiguous in the event that he might be unable to keep the papers from picking up the story.

Avery hung up. Just as Briggs sighed relief and put down the phone, Harry Calahan came strutting into the office, a broad grin extending across his face. With him was Early Smith. Briggs contemplated Harry's cocky face for a long moment in dead silence and then, when he could no longer contain himself, slammed the desk with a fist and shot up on his feet.

"You endangered an entire investigation," he began, tightening the fist. He was so angry that he gulped and had to start over. "You endangered an entire investigation last night, Calahan! By trying to push something that shouldn't have been pushed!"

Harry shrugged. His nonchalance caused Briggs to become entirely undone.

"Calahan, goddamnit, you blew the whole Imperial stakeout! Instead of keeping him under surveillance, like I told you to, you had to go and harass him. Now I want to know what the hell you have to say about that, and quick!"

"Nothing," Harry said.

Briggs was startled. "Is that what I'm supposed to tell Avery?" he said, gritting his teeth.

"Tell him it's not Imperial."

"What do you mean?" Briggs demanded.

"I mean, Briggs, that Imperial is not responsible for these murders, just like I told you yesterday. Now when are we going to stop wasting time?"

"Calahan, I—"

"Briggs, the man we're after is a traffic cop."

That bombshell fell to an extended beat of silence in the room. Both Briggs and Early were stupefied.

"A COP! A TRAFFIC COP!" Briggs became delirious. "Are you out of your mind, Calahan? You expect me to believe that a cop, a traffic cop, is knocking off all the top criminals in the city?"

"That's right."

"Who?" Early asked, wide-eyed.

"Charlie McCoy, I'm sorry to say He's ready for the rubber gun squad. He even tried to kill himself."

Early was speechless, Briggs stunned. Harry measured their reactions, but didn't say anything further until after a moment's silence, when he added, "He's my friend."

Briggs sat down, staring into space. In a tone of voice considerably softer than the one he'd started out using, though still somewhat harsh, he turned to Harry and said, "Calahan, Guzman was hit while you were playing your games with Imperial. A cop was killed. It was . . . Charlie McCoy."

Harry's face fell limp. "McCoy?" was all he could say.

"Yes," Briggs affirmed. "McCoy."

Harry's eyes grew abstracted and he shook his head.

"Now listen to me, Calahan. The only reason I don't bust you in the bag this very minute is that I know the two of you were close friends. He had kids, didn't he?"

Harry whispered, "Yes."

"I'm sorry," Briggs said sincerely.

Harry stood silently, still shaking his head. Finally he asked Briggs, "Who reported it?"

"A patrolman. Ben Davis."

"Davis!" He was stunned. "What about the stakeout team? DiGorgio's a good man."

"It was just one of those coincidences," Briggs explained. "Davis was going by when he heard the shots. McCoy was already dead when he got inside."

"Were there any witnesses?" Harry asked.

"None," Briggs replied.

"Are you sure?" Harry persisted.

"We checked it out thoroughly, Harry," Briggs said. "Not one."

"Jesus." Harry seemed unable to stop shaking his head. "I'd like to go call Carol McCoy."

"Go ahead," Briggs told him.

Harry turned and started for the door. Briggs called out after him, "Harry—if it means anything to you coming from me—I'm sorry about Charlie. But it's Imperial, believe me. It is. I'll have a warrant in forty-eight hours. You can pick him up. He's all yours."

Harry hesitated for a moment, then left. Early followed.

They walked in silence through the corridor to the elevator.

Early pushed the button and said, "I'm sorry, Harry." Just as he said this, the elevator doors opened and out stepped Ben Davis in uniform.

Silently and with an inscrutable look, Harry measured the man.

· Davis's face turned a pink shade and he gulped. "I'm sorry, sir," he said to Harry. "If I had come by sooner— McCoy might still be alive. I heard he was your friend. He didn't deserve to get it like that."

"Nobody does," Harry said softly. "That's what we get paid for."

"If there's anything I can do?" Davis offered. "I feel responsible in some way."

Harry just looked at him blankly and stepped into the elevator. Davis turned down the hall toward Briggs's office.

In the elevator Harry said to himself, allowing Early to overhear, "I still think it's a cop."

Chapter 19

The whine of the jet engines drowned out the rumbling forklift that raised Charlie McCoy's casket up to the cargo hold of the plane. Two ground men pulled the coffin inside and slid it into place with the other baggage. While some passengers were still boarding the flight, others, already in their seats, were getting settled. A few seated passengers, craning their necks, stared curiously at a man and woman standing near the boarding gate.

The woman, Carol McCoy, was dressed in black and held a small folded flag in her hands. Though she appeared to be composed, grief was apparent in her face. The man standing next to her wore a saddened expression as he held her gently by the elbow.

"Thank you for coming, Harry." She barely managed to get the words out.

"You sure about leaving, Carol?" Harry asked.

"I think it's the best thing," she said.

He smiled faintly. "That means I'm not going to have anywhere to go for a sit-down dinner anymore."

Carol returned a weak smile.

"I'm going to miss you," Harry said.

She rose on the tip of her toes to kiss him on the cheek. "I never did like it out here anyway," she said. She paused, trying hard to laugh, and added, "I always liked the change of seasons back East. I'll take him . . . home. It's time we went home. . . . Oh Christ, Harry, oh . . ."

She broke off, crying, and buried her face in Harry's jacket. Harry, guiding her with an arm around her shoulder, helped her toward the ramp. She pulled away gently and looked at him with wet eyes, unable to say anything.

"It's okay, Carol."

"Oh, Harry," was all she could manage, again erupting in tears.

He took her in his arms and patted her on the back.

"I'm sorry," she apologized, sobbing.

"No need, Carol."

As they held their affectionate embrace, Ben Davis walked past. He had Carol's daughter in one arm and her two young sons by his side, leading them up the ramp into the plane. When Carol spotted him she regained her composure and smiled appreciatively.

"It's so nice of that young man to help us," she told Harry.

"Yeh," Harry replied.

"Well, Harry," Carol sighed, fully collecting herself, "I guess this is it. Good-bye. We'll miss you."

They stood there, staring into each other's eyes, as two women with carry-on luggage pushed by. She kissed him one last time on the cheek, and, fighting back another tearful outburst, turned around and hurried up the ramp. When she turned around to wave from the door, he saw tears flowing from her eyes again.

Harry shouted something consoling to her but it was lost in the whine of the engines.

He saw the kids waving to him from inside the cabin. He waved back and smiled until they disappeared from the window. He looked all around, sniffing the air, biting his lip. Dusk was just settling over the airport.

Davis emerged from the plane and came down the ramp.

"Thanks," Harry told him over the roar of the plane. "You didn't have to do this."

"If I'd just come by sooner, McCoy might still be alive," Davis replied. "He didn't deserve to get it like that. It's the least I could do."

Harry gave him an unreadable look.

Chapter 20

On the way back to town from the airport, Ben Davis ran out of cigarettes. He asked Harry whether he'd mind pulling off the freeway for a minute to buy a fresh pack. Though Harry was eager to get to the target range for a final practice round before the annual shooting contests scheduled to take place the next day, he said, "Okay, but let's make it quick."

Harry took the next exit and drove two blocks to one of his haunts—the Castle Lane Bowling Alley—where he knew there was a cigarette machine. When they got there, Harry stopped in front and shut off the engine.

"What the hell, Davis, let's have a quick beer," he proposed.

"That's a fine idea, sir," Davis countered.

Harry locked the car and the two men walked to the building, finding it bustling with activity. All the lanes were occupied. The room reverberated with the rumble of bowling balls and the clatter of falling pins. Just as Harry and Davis stepped into the doorway they came up against a group of four young people who were on their way out. Two were girls, one a blond and the other a brunette, both stunning and neither more than eighteen years old. They were accompanied by two boys, who appeared to be a few years older. One of the boys was a frail but handsome black lad, while the other was white and gangly.

"This place smells like kids tonight," Harry observed sardonically for all to hear.

Davis, who in some ways still thought of himself as a "kid," laughed. But he was distracted when the blond girl, in passing him, brushed up against his shoulder—an accident, it seemed. It nonetheless provided the young

111

patrolman with an opportunity to turn and clock her figure. Harry walked on ahead, toward the bar.

As Davis stared at the last of the blond's disappearing legs, he was slammed off balance by two men rushing out of the building in a great hurry. One of the men was large and scar-faced and the other was small and stocky with greased hair. Both wore faded workclothes, and jackets which proclaimed boldly across the backs: OLYMPIC CARPETS.

Davis regained his balance and, sensing something ominous from their gait, started after them. When he reached the street he spotted them rushing around the corner. He took off after them, running hard. He rounded the corner and followed them halfway down the next block and into an alley which cut around the back of the bowling alley. When he neared the end of the alley he heard the sounds of a struggle which seemed to be taking place in a used-car lot across the street.

Suddenly two figures came racing toward him, screaming for help. When they ran under a streetlight he immediately recognized them as the same brunette and the white boy he had just seen leaving the bowling alley. Their faces were locked in terror. The boy shouted something, but it was drowned out by a passing truck. Not until the boy repeated himself a second time, even more urgently, could Davis decipher the breathless message:

"He has a heart condition!" the boy panted hysterically. "They'll kill him!"

Davis responded instantly by breaking into a dead run to the used-car lot, where he found the two Olympic Carpet men beating the black boy bloody. They had the boy pinned to the ground. He was bleeding heavily and gasping for breath.

The large scar-faced man spotted the uniform and lunged at Davis with a lethal-looking carpet-cutting knife. With no loss of grace in his stride, Davis backed around and kicked the man full in the face, sending him reeling backwards, stunned, spinning to the pavement.

His cohort, the small, stocky man, took off like a shot from a gun, darting into the street, dodging cars. Davis bounded after him, running furiously. The chase snarled traffic; the sounds of cars screeching and horns blaring abruptly filled the night. A cab swerved crazily in front of Davis, just missing him.

The small man was trapped between two sliding cars when Davis saw him. The rookie patrolman picked up a wire trash basket and heaved it in his direction. Trash spewed all over the street and onto the cars.

The basket caught the short man off guard, hitting him square in the abdomen. His feet suddenly skidded out from under him and he tumbled forward, smashing into a parked Oldsmobile. Before he could get back up, Davis was all over him.

He grabbed the man's collar with both hands and bashed his head mercilessly into the car window, shattering glass. The man groaned in a sickly fashion and fell on all fours, staggering over himself, to the ground. Davis picked him up by his hair and rammed the man's head into the fender, denting the steel.

Just as he did so, the large man recovered and scrambled for his knife, a few feet away.

Suddenly Harry appeared from the dark shadows, a bottle of beer in his hand.

As the large scar-faced man rushed Davis with the carpet knife, Harry swung the beer bottle down on his head. The bottle shattered into an explosion of suds and glass. The man fell over backwards, hands over eyes. Harry finished him off by balling both fists into a club and using it to cave in the man's gut. The man started to rise on his knees, but then fell forward. By the time his face smashed into the pavement he was out. Harry snapped a pair of cuffs on his leg and locked the man to the door handle of a car.

He then rushed to the black boy who lay sprawled by a row of gleaming used cars. Finding the boy's eyes rolled all the way back in his head, Harry dropped to the ground and pounded his chest furiously, swearing inwardly under his breath. The boy did not move. Harry put an ear to the chest. There was no sound. The boy was dead.

Turning, Harry spotted Davis still banging the other

man's head into the fender, though the man was no longer conscious. The fender was so dented it looked as if the car had been in an accident.

Harry watched as Davis drew a gun from his holster and, bringing the man up by his collar, proceeded to crack his skull with the butt. When he was finished, Davis tossed the body to the pavement, smirking at it contemptuously.

Harry came running up. He stared down at the bloodied man and then looked Davis straight in the eyes.

"He was already out before you did that," Harry said from behind gritted teeth.

"I know," Davis started, out of breath.

Harry grew wide-eyed.

Davis caught his breath and explained, "We hate those bastards."

"We?" Harry demanded.

But before Davis could reply, the brunette teenage girl came running up and found the black boy lying dead on the pavement. She let out a long piercing scream and fell to his body, sobbing. The blond girl kneeled at her side, trembling and grief-stricken.

"Oh my God, oh my God," she cried.

The white boy stood over them, watching, scared and humiliated.

Harry turned away from Davis and walked up to the brunette, kneeling to talk to her.

"Police," he said. "Is he your boy friend?"

Without turning she said, "Yes," in a cracked voice.

"I'm sorry," Harry told her.

The girl burst into tears. Sobbing, she rose up into the blond's arms. Harry took off his jacket and covered the dead boy's face. On one sleeve of the jacket was the black armband he had worn that afternoon to Charlie McCoy's funeral.

Meanwhile, a crowd began to collect at the scene, including passers-by and a number of people from the bowling alley, many of them, as Harry had been, still holding drinks in their hands. In the midst of the commotion, the white boy suddenly became hysterical.

"Oh God! Oh God!" he shrieked. "What are we going

to tell his family? Oh God! I should have stayed to help him, oh God. I wanted to—I wanted to help—oh God—I didn't mean to run away—I hate violence."

The crowd was stunned. The boy broke down in tears, losing all control. Harry looked at him with nothing to say. Davis, however, was moved to respond in a rather odd and startling manner. He walked up to the boy and lectured him, in a voice loud enough for all to hear, "How much more will it take to get people like you upset enough to face violence?"

The boy bolted up, shocked.

Davis turned and proceeded to address the entire crowd, his voice rising. "How much longer do you people intend to put up with these two-bit criminals? How much longer do you think you can run away from violence before this sort of thing happens to you? How much longer will you be indifferent? HOW MUCH LONGER?"

On this last note, Davis realized how loudly he was shouting, and he stopped, flushing with embarrassment.

Harry remained unblinking, taking it all in.

Chapter 21

A target silhouette of a gunman popped up in a window frame. Three shots rang out, two of which plugged the target's vital area while the other veered a couple of inches too high. The target dropped.

In a second window another target popped up—this one a facsimile of a policeman. No shot was fired.

Then suddenly two more bad guys appeared in another window, and the target was met by a fusillade of shots. Two of the bullets hit one figurine and the others went astray, leaving the second bad guy still standing.

The man doing the shooting was Detective Sal Di-Gorgio. When he finished, he stood up from behind a barricade, opening the cylinder on his service revolver. Off to one side, a scorekeeper tallied his score and placed it on a large blackboard under the event designated "Practical Police Course—Combat."

It was Sunday and the outdoor target range was jammed with cops. Some were in uniform, but most had come in their street clothes. The atmosphere was festive, as it usually was for the annual event. Policemen and their families were milling about everywhere, enjoying themselves, watching, drinking, talking. The talk was mostly about guns and loads and about Dirty Harry, who was something of a legend in these contests. He almost never lost an event he entered.

The rangemaster approved the DiGorgio score, then walked to the microphone.

"The next shooter is Calahan," he announced. "Davis on deck."

Harry Calahan stepped to the firing line wearing a nylon windbreaker, over which a shoulder holster was strapped tightly. In the holster was his large .44 Magnum.

The firing line consisted of several short walls and barricades. An old junk car was off to one side. Harry took a deep breath.

"All right," the rangemaster announced into the microphone, "you've got thirty shots permissible. Targets will be scored on time as well as hits. You may pick the shots you prefer. It's your gunfire. Are you ready?"

Harry spread his legs apart and said, "Ready."

"Load."

He jammed in a speedloader.

"Holster."

Harry holstered the .44.

"Ready on the left," the rangemaster said. "Ready on the right. Ready on the firing line?"

"Ready," Harry replied.

"Go!"

All at once several targets popped up. Harry whipped out his gun and got off a single shot from the hip, which instantly felled a bad-guy figurine. Then he swung past a good guy and brought the gun up to a two-handed position, plugging two more shots into a second bad guy. He shifted the gun to combat position, spun around behind a wall, shooting.

He then ejected, loaded in another speedloader, and came out firing again as he darted for the car. In the sprint from the wall to the car he unloaded an entire clip; each shot took down a target.

He crouched behind the jalopy, loaded again, came up, and, bracing himself against a window, aimed through the car. In spite of the incredible speed with which he triggered the gun, he remained deadly accurate. The targets rose and fell in a steady progression, each one plugged at least once in a vital area.

When he finished, people cheered on all sides, and Harry walked off the firing line. Several men crowded around him, patting him on the shoulder, shaking his hand. It seemed almost certain, barring any miracle performance by Davis, that once again Dirty Harry would be the undisputed champion in the combat event.

"You took everybody's pants down with that score,

117

"Harry," Sal DiGiorgio said, approaching with an outstretched hand. "I've never seen you smoother."

"Thanks, Sal."

"Uh, by the way, Harry," DiGiorgio took him by the elbow, "I've been meaning to tell you personally how sorry I am about your pal Charlie."

The mention of McCoy took the smile off Harry's face. "How in the hell did this kid Davis get in there before you, Sal?" Harry asked searchingly. "You were right there, across the street."

"Harry," DiGiorgio threw his hands up, "I don't have a goddamn notion of an idea how he did it. He came out of nowhere. We actually *saw* McCoy go in, but not Davis. And we got into that garage before you could spit, Harry! Only thing I can figure is maybe I'm getting slow in my old age."

As DiGiorgio finished talking, Phil Sweet walked up, smiling. The patrolman offered Harry his hand. After a slight hesitation, Harry accepted.

"Inspector Calahan," Sweet bellowed, "I'd like to be one of the first to congratulate you on what I think will be the winning score. You shaded me by a full seven points. Seems only one guy's got a chance on you now in the combine and that," he nodded toward the firing line, "is Davis."

The rangemaster had finished recording Harry's score and preparing for the next set-up as Ben Davis took a stance at the firing line, his eyes strangely cold. Harry, Sweet and DiGiorgio all turned to watch.

"Load," came the voice of the rangemaster.

Davis withdrew his pistol and loaded it. Harry found himself studying the process with more than casual interest. Davis's pistol had a long target barrel, the sort not normally found on a service pistol.

"Holster."

Davis dropped the gun back into the holster and steadied his legs.

"Ready on the right. Ready on the left. Ready on the firing line?"

"Ready!" Davis yelled out.

"GO!"

Davis whipped the gun out of the holster and started blasting. He was all concentration, hands expertly maneuvering the gun, drilling one target after another dead center. He reloaded, felled a second round of targets with equal proficiency, and then after one more expert round the whole target range fell silent in awe for a brief moment as the rangemaster walked to the blackboard to record Davis's score.

"I think that kid might have beat you, Harry," DiGorgio said, speaking from the corner of his mouth in a low, discreet voice.

"I had a bad day—happens," Harry told him.

Grimes and Astrachan joined Sweet, and all grinned broadly as they watched the rangemaster pick up the chalk.

Davis's official recorded score brought a large collective gasp from the crowd. This was followed by an excited round of applause and much cheering. Davis had beaten Harry by four points.

Harry remained expressionless. Though there were folks in the crowd who may have mistaken this lack of response for bad sportsmanship, the fact of the matter was that Harry was deeply preoccupied with other thoughts.

Davis smiled and wiped his brow. The rangemaster walked up to Harry.

"Harry," said the rangemaster, amazement in his voice, "looks like he edged you on this one, but your scores even up for overall champion. For the shoot-off you have the choice: bull's-eye or combat?"

"Combat," Harry said. His face continued to lack expression.

The rangemaster headed back up to the microphone and announced, "Ladies and gentlemen, we have a tie for overall champion. Our next and final event will be the shoot-off between Harry Calahan and Ben Davis."

The crowd buzzed with anticipation.

"Inspector Calahan has chosen combat as the event,"

the rangemaster continued. Turning to Davis, he asked, "Three targets—six shots, timed?"

"That sounds good," Davis replied.

"Any way he wants it," Harry called out tightly. His movements became very stiff.

"Okay. Who's going to lead off?" the rangemaster asked.

"I will," Davis grinned. "Before I get cold."

Everyone else stepped back, leaving Davis and Harry alone on the firing line. Davis wiped his hands on his jeans, cracked his fingers and then limbered his body.

"The clock will be activated by your voice," the rangemaster told him. A microphone dangled on a stick behind the marksman.

"Are you ready, sir?" the rangemaster proceeded.

"Ready," Davis replied.

"Load. Remember now, six shots, rapid-fire."

Davis loaded.

"Holster your weapon."

Davis holstered the gun.

"Ready on the right, ready on the left, ready on the firing line?"

"START!" Davis shouted.

He drew his gun and fired smoothly at the first target, a bad guy. Then he plugged the target one more time, to be sure, allowing the next figurine, a good guy, to pass. He emptied the four remaining shots into the third target, another bad guy, and pulled the gun up out of recoil.

"Out!" he shouted, raising the gun over his head.

Sweet, Grimes and Astrachan whistled their approval. The crowd followed suit by cheering wildly. When the applause died, the stands were buzzing with conversation. It seemed, for the first time in memory, that Harry Calahan had met his match on the target range.

"Time: two point four seconds," the rangemaster said, looking up from his stopwatch. "Score: perfect."

Harry walked up, his eyes riveted into Davis. Davis smiled enigmatically.

"Good luck, sir," he told Harry.

Harry nodded, indicating that he doubted he would

need it, and went straight up to the line, opening the .44 at his side.

"Ready, Harry?" the rangemaster inquired.

"Ready."

"Load. Six shots rapid-fire."

Harry loaded.

"Holster your weapon."

Harry holstered the gun and loosened his shoulders. Davis moved to the sidelines. He was all concentration on Harry. Harry was all concentration on the targets.

The rangemaster gave the final cue: "Ready on the right, ready on the left, ready on the firing line—"

"Now," Harry said, not very loudly.

He whipped his gun out as three targets snapped up simultaneously. The .44 roared out a rapid-fire six shots, two in each target, incredibly fast. So fast, in fact, that the six shots sounded like one long one. But unfortunately on his final shot his hand had slipped a fraction, just enough to throw the shot away. He pulled the gun out of recoil. The crowd sat stunned.

Sal DiGorgio's jaw dropped. It almost seemed to him that Harry had deliberately flubbed the final shot.

"Good guy! Good guy!" a voice cried out from the stands. "The last one he hit was a good guy!"

The rangemaster's voice came amplified: "Time: one point eight seconds. But . . . I'm sorry, Harry . . . you hit a good guy. The new champion—Ben Davis."

The crowd cheered and rushed Davis from all sides. Davis, however, broke abruptly from his admirers and hurried over to Harry, hand outstretched.

Harry accepted the handshake.

"You had a bad break," Davis told him. "I don't really deserve it."

"You won, didn't you?" Harry shrugged.

"Well, yes, but—"

"But nothing. Winning is all that matters, isn't it?"

"Yes, sir, I guess so."

Harry pointed a finger at Davis's pistol, asking, "Can I try it?"

"Sure thing," Davis replied eagerly. "Help yourself. It's got a custom barrel and sights."

Harry took the gun in hand and felt the weight. "It's heavier than it looks," he commented.

"I like the balance," Davis said. "It's stable when you get on to it."

Harry allowed, "I've never seen one like it before."

"Give it a try."

"Sure you don't mind?"

"Not at all, sir."

"Okay, Chester," Harry called to the rangemaster. "Once more."

There was a slight grin on Harry's face as he stepped up to the firing line and loaded the gun. He seemed immensely relaxed.

"Ready on the firing line," the rangemaster called.

Harry drew the gun and fired. The first shot was lost in the wood of the target frame, but the next five drilled a nice neat pattern into the silhouette of a bad guy. When he finished shooting, Harry wiped his mouth with the back of his hand and gave the gun back to Davis.

"I lost the first one," Harry explained.

"You get used to it," Davis said.

"How's that?" Harry asked, pretending not to hear.

"You get used to it, sir."

"Yeh," Harry mused, half to himself. "I can see how you would."

Davis smiled and holstered the gun. He started to say something, but swallowed it before he did.

Later that night, when the outdoor target range was deserted, Harry went back with a flashlight. He scanned a number of targets until he found the one he was looking for. He dug a knife into the target's wooden frame and pulled out the slug he'd fired there earlier in the day with Davis's gun.

Chapter 22

Though the hour was late, Harry Calahan went directly from the outdoor target range to the ballistics lab. Briggs had assigned him to yet another innocuous stakeout that night, but Harry was in no hurry to get there. He'd told Early that he wanted to check out something else first in the ballistics lab, and had asked his partner to wait for him in the cafeteria of the police building.

"Harry, it'll be our ass if Briggs ever finds out," Early admonished.

"Don't worry," was all Harry would say.

"At least tell me what you're up to," Early insisted.

"Not yet," Harry replied.

Finding the ballistics lab closed and empty, Harry located the light switch and took a seat at a microscope. For several minutes he sat there examining the deep-cut rifling on the bullet he'd fired at the target range, then he got up and went to a cabinet to look for the slugs that the mortician had pulled out of Charlie McCoy. Finding the correct tray, he took out a slug and returned with it to the microscope, where he examined it very carefully, back to back with the slug he'd planted in the wood of the target frame with Davis's Smith and Wesson. The bullets matched up almost identically. He looked up from the microscope and stared into a blank wall. He must have been in that position for quite some time, because after a while Early stormed in.

"Hey!" Early protested. "You said five minutes. It's almost a half hour!"

"Really," Harry said, getting up from the microscope. He put his slug in his pocket, and returned the other to the tray where he'd found it.

"Christ, Harry." Early was simply exasperated. "Will you please tell me what this is all about?"

"I'm ready," Harry replied. "What time is it?"

"Ten before midnight."

"Let's call it a night." Harry led the way to the door, cutting the lights.

"Harry, are you crazy? We've got that stakeout on—"

"It's a waste of time."

"You may be right, but Briggs doesn't think so."

"I don't care what Briggs thinks—if he thinks at all."

"Harry—are you on to something?"

"I may be."

"What? A lead?"

"What you don't know can't hurt you, Smith. Go home and meet me here at eight sharp in the morning."

After dropping Early off in the lobby, Harry took the elevator up to the fifth floor and spent much of the remainder of the night reading four files in the personnel office.

The first was Thomas Astrachan, twenty-three, known to everyone by the nickname "Red," for his auburn hair. From his file, Harry learned that Astrachan had grown up in Houston, where he'd maintained an average high-school record and played guard on the basketball team. He had spent two years at Ohio State University, but then in the midst of the Vietnam build-up had enlisted in the Special Forces. After his discharge he came to San Francisco and spent a summer working as a check-out man in Marina Safeway before applying to the police department. He attached a statement to his application in which he detailed his reasons for wanting to be a policeman. Harry read it four times:

"I think that working as a police officer would be the logical extension of my experience as Special Forces Ranger in the Republic of Vietnam. The real danger confronting our nation today no longer comes from Russia or China or their allies, but from the subversives living right within our midst. By subversives I do not mean only political radicals, although I do include them, but I also mean the criminal element who undercut our democracy and freedom by their contempt for our laws. The recent relaxation of criminal rights by the Supreme Court has created a condition in our nation today where criminals can roam the streets without fear of capture or punishment. This situation is very unhealthy, and I would be the sort of police officer who took this into consideration at all times."

Though Harry could have felt comfortable with those same words in his own mouth, there was something in Astrachan's tone that disturbed him, though he wasn't sure of what it was. He searched through Astrachan's service record for some clue, but found the file chock full of nothing but sterling attributes. It seemed that everybody liked Red Astrachan, especially his superiors, who maintained that he was a conscientious, obedient soldier, competent to carry out even the most delicate assignments.

After he finished with Astrachan, Harry went on to get acquainted with John Grimes, twenty-seven, whose records gave nothing to indicate why he had chosen police work as a profession, other than that he, like his pal Astrachan, was a veteran of the Special Forces.

Grimes had grown up in Scranton, Pa., and had attended parochial schools there until he'd entered college. His was a biography of the athlete-scholar. He had been a reliable, if not outstanding, quarterback on the college football team, but a knee injury during the final game of the final season had made him less than desirable as a potential property for the professional football leagues. Throughout his college career he had been a dean's list student and upon graduation had been contemplating law school when he decided instead to join the army. From what Harry could determine in searching his service record, Grimes had been an unexceptional soldier, though seemingly a brave one. He had applied to and was accepted by the Special Forces, and it was in his stint there, as Harry already knew, that he met Astrachan as well as the two other musketeers.

He, Astrachan and Sweet, according to a document

Harry found in Grimes's file, had during one period of their employment with the Defense Department served as informants who reported on fellow soldiers who smoked marijuana. Grimes himself had spent some time working directly for intelligence sources in the army, though the exact nature of this association was not evident from the documents in the personnel files.

A personnel interviewer for the police department, however, had noted in a report in Grimes's file that the young man claimed to have done some "sensitive infiltration work for the army concerning traitors and saboteurs." In the same report the interviewer also observed, "This young man has what it takes to make a good police officer. He is college-educated and upset by the direction in which his generation is going. He shows an especially shrewd manner of action and would be very effective in handling rowdy elements. He feels a strong obligation to help society and he says that, with the crime rate what it is, there is no better way to do so than as an officer of the law."

Grimes came through the police academy with honors, and in his ten months on the force it seemed he had drawn nothing but favorable comments in the monthly efficiency and behavior reports filed by his superiors.

There was, ultimately, only one tiny item in the entire Grimes file that made Harry so much as raise an eyebrow. This was a small tidbit revealing that it had been Grimes who first reported the recent murder of the mobsters in Tiburon. Harry pondered this for several minutes before closing the file and opening the next one—Phil Sweet.

Philip Sweet, twenty-five, from Baton Rouge, La., had made his way to the Special Forces through a college ROTC program. He had attended Louisiana State University and received a liberal arts degree. Scholastically, he was an average student. His father served a term as Mayor of Oakdale, but decided against campaigning for re-election in favor of a job working on an offshore oil rig. His mother was extremely active in community and church affairs. Sweet had had a very stringent Catholic upbringing. This led him to seek psychiatric counseling while attending LSU, because he had suffered guilt trauma upon having his first sexual relations with a young foreign student from Sweden.

Harry found his service record relatively unblemished, with the exception of one minor infraction. One night in a Bavarian tavern on the outskirts of a large American army base, where he was undergoing special unspecified training, Sweet was one of two dozen soldiers arrested by MPs in a drunken brawl. He was administratively disciplined for taking part in the brawl, receiving a suspended sentence and six months' probation. Though regarded by practically everybody as a most pleasant fellow, Sweet was, at times, various items in the file revealed, a discipline problem; he was known to occasionally lapse from his amiable demeanor into a state where he was overcome by a gruesome temper.

However, in the larger picture, Sweet, like Astrachan, seemed to have been an outstanding soldier. He'd won a long string of medals for valor and courage in various Vietnam campaigns, and had been widely regarded in his unit for his talents in persuading taciturn enemy soldiers to talk. However, as far as his stint with military intelligence was concerned, the details were sparse.

Sweet's application to the police department contained a letter of recommendation from a state legislator in Louisiana, which said, in part, "This young man, who has served his country so well on the battlefield, would make an exceptionally fine police officer. He has respect for our great American institutions and will uphold them with honor on the police force in the same way he has done on the battlefield. It should be noted that he comes from a fine family with a long history of public service. In sum, I feel that young Mr. Sweet's ambition to become an officer of the law is a fine example of how military service can and will better the young men in our country."

Another item that aroused Harry's interest somewhat was a newspaper clipping about Phil Sweet's activities in an organization of veterans that supported the Indo-China war. Curiously enough, Sweet was quoted in the article as contending he felt that "in addition to the radicals who

127

undermine the war effort, I am equally opposed to the hard-core criminal elements in this country who are getting away with murder due to a permissiveness in the judicial system."

Then there was Ben Davis. His file, Harry discovered, was the slimmest of all. He had grown up in Michigan as an orphan and enlisted in the army when he was eighteen. He was discharged eight years later, at the age of twenty-six, after two back-to-back tours of duty in Vietnam. He had intended to re-enlist for a third time, but when the decision was made to wind down the war he decided to come home. He traveled from city to city looking for a job until he arrived in San Francisco, where he found his three closest pals from the army working for the San Francisco Police Department.

Davis applied too and was accepted. He graduated from the police academy the highest in his class. There was a special evaluation report in his file from Detective Lieutenant Neil Briggs, which described Davis as "the most outstanding young officer to join the department in years, and one from whom we can expect great things."

After reading that, Harry closed the file and went home.

Chapter 23

When Harry Calahan walked into Briggs's office the following morning, the lieutenant, as usual, was working two phones. Seeing Harry, he hung up on one line and barked a parting shot into the other: "Thanks, Jim. Now we'll grab those animals with their pants down."

He set down the second phone and motioned for Harry to have a seat. There was something uncharacteristically affable about Briggs's manner, which led Harry to conclude that he knew nothing yet about how Inspectors Calahan and Smith had neglected to perform their stakeout responsibilities the previous night.

"Harry," Briggs started excitedly, "I just tried calling you at home."

"I overslept."

"Good news: we've got our search warrants and multiple charges. We're going to make a citywide raid tomorrow morning. Imperial is all yours. Just don't take him out head first, Harry. That's all I ask."

"I appreciate this, Briggs—"

"It wasn't easy."

"—but maybe you better come down to the ballistics lab with me first."

Briggs sprung up in his swivel chair. "What? You got a lead?"

"Maybe."

"I think you'll find more leads than you can shake a stick at tomorrow morning."

"Let's you and I go shake a stick at one right now, Briggs."

Briggs shrugged and got up. "Let's go."

The lab technician, Walter Smathers, was at his desk, a bagel in his mouth, his hands at work snapping off the plas-

9   129

tic top of a container of steaming coffee. Looking up, he saw Briggs and Calahan enter the lab.

"Good morning, sir. Good morning, Harry," he said, as best as he could manage, through the bagel.

"Good morning, Walter," Briggs replied.

"Walter," Harry walked up to him, "would you get me those slugs they took out of Charlie McCoy, please?"

"Sure thing." Walter put the bagel down on his desk and went to a cabinet where he removed a tray labeled ".357 Magnum slugs—Charles McCoy." He handed it to Harry.

"Okay, now get me the slugs on Carmine Ricca and the pimp," Harry said.

"They're not here," Briggs answered for Smathers. "The federal boys have 'em."

"They do, huh? Since when?"

"Oh, they've had them a couple of days now," Briggs replied offhandedly.

"Okay, Walter," Harry continued, "then get me some of that lead they took out of those boys in Tiburon."

"Federal boys have that, too, I'm afraid." Briggs again did the answering.

"Jesus," Harry said, disturbed. After a concentrated moment of deep thought he walked across the room and situated himself at a microscope, asking Walter if he'd mind going out for a few minutes.

"What the hell for?" It was Briggs who asked.

"It's okay," Walter injected, leaving with his bagel and coffee, "I'm not sensitive."

Harry took a bullet from the tray and set it up under the microscope. Then he took a second bullet out of his pocket and placed it beside it.

As he had done the night before, Harry rotated each slug until he was reminded of how the rifling marks and striations matched up almost identically on all sides. After a minute or so, in which Briggs hovered over him impatiently, Harry got up and said, "Have a look."

Briggs poured his eyes into the microscope and held them there for an unusually long moment in which he said nothing and did not react. Then he pulled away to glance back at Harry.

He gathered his mouth together anxiously before he spoke. "Close," he said. "Real close."

"More than close," Harry proposed.

"Well, I don't know about that," Briggs allowed, getting up. "There are still a lot of lines that don't match up." His face showed weariness rather than satisfaction.

"Mmm," was all Harry would say. He gave Briggs a drilling look.

"Harry," Briggs reasoned, "all this proves is that these two bullets came out of barrels with a similar twist and depth of rifling. It really doesn't prove anything other than that."

Harry tore his eyes off Briggs and retrieved the bullets from under the microscope. He put one back in the tray and the other back in his pocket. Briggs appeared to be slightly jarred, watching.

Harry asked, "You think it would pass for evidence, Briggs?"

"As it is?" Briggs replied. "No. Definitely not.".

"Hmm," was Harry's reaction.

"But I'll tell you what," Briggs continued, "I'll have a full, complete comparison report made right away. No trouble." He held out his hand. "Let me see the bullet."

"Which bullet?"

"The one you just put in your pocket."

"Oh, this!" Harry dug it out of his pocket again, but just as Briggs reached for it, he flipped it casually into the air, caught it, and returned it to his pocket. "No, I think I'll just hold on to it, Briggs. I think you're probably right."

"I'll decide if I'm right."

"Well, it's not really necessary to run any comparison report. Not yet, anyway."

"What do you mean *yet?*" Briggs, growing haughty, wanted to know.

"I mean time will tell."

"Look, Calahan, cut out the games. Where did you get that slug?"

"Well, well, well. I was wondering when you might get

around to asking me that question, Briggs. A little more practice and you might even make it as a detective."

"Where did you get it, Calahan?"•

"I'd rather not say just yet."

"Goddamnit, Calahan, I said cut out the games. Whose side are you on, anyway?"

"Look—it's just a wild shot, is all." Harry slipped into a more reasonable tone of voice. "I could be wrong again —maybe even wronger than I was before. So just let me handle it my own way for a while."

"Calahan, you son of a—"

"Now hold your temper, Briggs. Please. If I told you once I told you a hundred times: a smart man should know his limitations. It applies in a lot of ways."

"Calahan, when this case is done, I give you my word, it's your ass."

"Sure, Briggs, sure. By the way, I want Davis and Sweet ·in my back-up squad tomorrow.":

"What!" Briggs was startled.

"You heard me. Davis and Sweet."

"For chrissakes, Calahan, I think you've finally lost your mind. Those guys are just rookies!"

"Okay—you scare me up anybody in this department who can shoot better than either of them—other than me —and maybe I'll use them instead."

"But they don't have the experience yet for a job as big as this one," Briggs protested.

"Nobody ever gets any experience in this business unless somebody sticks his neck out and gives them a chance first," Harry replied. "And I'm gonna give them that chance. Besides, Davis is now the new pistol champion."

"That doesn't mean a damn thing," Briggs yelled. "Suppose they panic and start shooting?"

"They won't," Harry assured him.

"But suppose they do?" Briggs insisted.

"Nothing wrong with shooting—if the right people get shot," Harry figured.

Briggs turned around and stormed out, muttering a string of vicious remarks under his breath.

After he left, Walter Smathers came back, asking, "What's with him, Harry?"

"I was just beginning to wonder that myself, Walter," Harry replied.

Chapter 24

It was a brisk Sunday morning in San Francisco, an hour before sunrise. In the parking lot at police headquarters, in the first rays of dawn, some twenty unmarked police cars were lined up in two even rows. Squads of uniformed police and plainclothesmen lugged heavy weapons from the building, placing them in the trunks of the automobiles. Within the hour a massive citywide raid was slated to get under way, with the purpose of swooping down on and rounding up the bay area's most notorious underworld characters.

The man in charge of the operation, Detective Lieutenant Neil Briggs, was in a buoyant mood as he roamed the lot, clipboard in hand, filling in each squad on the last-minute particulars of their assignment in the operation. Briggs had been up all night finalizing the plans.

Harry Calahan emerged from the police building with his partner, Early Smith, at his side. Harry caught a glimpse of Briggs making the rounds, and he tightened his jaw. He scanned the scene, searching for Phil Sweet and Ben Davis, and finally spotted them chatting together next to one of the unmarked cars.

"I have a special assignment for you," Harry quietly told Early as they walked along.

"Uh-oh."

"This is no joke, Smith. Listen to me and listen to me carefully." Harry spoke with eyes straight ahead. "I want you to keep your eyes on Sweet and Davis the whole time. Do you understand me?"

"What the hell for?" Early demanded. "Jesus, Harry, we're not about to go play kindergarten games."

"Don't ask me any questions. Just do what I say."

"But—"

"Just do it!"

Before Early could further protest, Briggs walked up and intercepted them.

"I don't know why I'm doing this for you, Calahan," he said coldly, "but I'm putting Davis and Sweet in your squad, as requested. Any funny business, and I warn you—"

"Save your breath, Briggs." Harry wasn't interested.

Briggs started to blow up again but caught himself in time. Fuming frustration through his nose, he asked, simply, "How you set, Calahan?"

Harry's reply was all business. "Two cars," he said. "We drive up quick. Davis and Sweet will make the arrest, with Smith covering. I'll be in the alley to catch anyone who tries to break and run for it. If there's going to be any trouble, that's where it'll take place."

"You fellas all set?" Briggs asked, turning to greet Sweet and Davis, who had just walked up.

"Yes, sir," Davis said.

"Yes, sir," Sweet said.

Then, together: "We appreciate this, lieutenant."

Briggs did not respond to their expressions of gratitude, but with thinly disguised hostility turned back to Harry, admonishing, "We're holding the other squads back until you've made your arrest. We figure Imperial is the most important one to net first. We wouldn't want to give him any chance to warn his friends. So don't pull any tricks, Calahan."

"Wouldn't think of it."

Briggs sneered and then turned to walk away, leaving Early with this bit of advice: "You know, I'd never walk up to a door with Calahan. Too many people don't like him."

Early threw his hands in the air, muttering, "Thanks! That sure does make me feel a whole lot better."

Briggs, without looking back, moved on to the next squad. Davis and Sweet seemed somewhat embarrassed.

"Okay," Harry boomed, "are you boys ready?"

"Yes, sir, we are." Davis spoke for both of them.

"Inspector Calahan," Sweet added, "we wanted to thank you for requesting us on your squad."

"Don't mention it."

"We won't disappoint you," Davis promised.

"I'm counting on that," Harry said. "Let's go."

Harry drove one car himself. Early, Sweet and Davis followed in a second car. The drive took only ten minutes, but by the time they arrived the sky had already lightened considerably, and daybreak was at hand. However, the streets were still quiet and deserted, with almost no traffic in sight.

Harry pulled to a stop near an alley leading to the warehouse. Early stopped the other car a few feet away, directly in front of the building. Harry got out of the car and headed into the alley, where he saw a Buick parked next to a back door. He moved to conceal himself behind a garbage can when he heard a faint but persistent ring of a telephone inside the warehouse.

Chapter 25

Frank Imperial sat overflowing out of an overstuffed chair, a serving platter of a dozen fried eggs resting on his lap, a loaf of bread and a cardboard container of milk on the floor beside him. He used one hand to eat while employing the other to clutch the comics section of the Sunday paper. When the phone started to ring, he took a long pull on the milk, put it down, and grabbed a slice of bread to mop up the egg juice on his plate. He didn't appear to be even slightly curious as to who might be calling him at such an early hour.

In another corner of the room four burly-looking men were also having breakfast, though somewhat more conventionally. They were sitting at a table, eating from plates rather than platters. A shotgun rested against the table and each man had a pistol resting near his napkin. At the sound of the phone they all turned and shot looks at Imperial, but found him too engrossed in Dick Tracy to indicate whether or not he wanted it answered. They looked from him to one another, shrugged, and picked up their forks again in silence. After a few seconds or so, the phone still ringing, Imperial, without looking up from the comics, raised a hand in which he held a piece of bread and motioned for somebody to answer.

As soon as he did this, one of the men jumped up and grabbed the phone, nearly tripping over a packing box for a new Thompson stock submachine model. He put the receiver to his ear, wiping his mouth with a sleeve. Suddenly his eyes grew large. After listening wide-eyed and in silence for a moment, he demanded, "Who is this? I said who the hell is this? You better tell me who you are! You sonofabitch, I'll bend your ass backwards if I ever lay hands on you, you goddamn no good—"

At that, the caller apparently hung up, leaving the man standing there, staring dumbfoundedly into the receiver.

The three other men at the table spun around in their chairs at once. Imperial looked up, asking through a mouthful of eggs, "What was that, Nicky?"

Nicky put the receiver down and planted his stunned eyes on the door. He spoke quickly. "Somebody just said we're gonna be hit in two minutes!"

"WHAT!" exclaimed one of the men at the table.

Nicky added, "This guy said they'll be dressed as cops."

All eyes fixed on Imperial, who suddenly lost his appetite for both eggs and comics. He stood up and demanded, "Did it sound like anyone you know, Nicky?"

"No, Frank, I couldn't tell. The guy only said we'll be hit in two minutes and they'll be dressed as cops. He wouldn't say who he was. He just hung up."

There was a beat of silence as Imperial hauled his bulk around the chair and then, in a fit of temper, hurled his platter of eggs at the TV set, causing the picture tube to blow apart in a hail of shattering glass, with eggs sliding and dripping all over the console. He lumbered to the table, faced the men, and slammed his fist into the wood, causing the plates to rattle.

"All right," he snarled. "Nicky, you take the front door, and, Vance, take the garage door. You two get over there by the windows. We ain't taking no chances."

"But, Frank, what if they really are cops?" Vance dared to ask. "It could be a set-up," he added timidly.

Vance's three colleagues, failing to share his doubts, scrambled to their posts, guns in hands. One stopped at the packing box and removed the Thompson submachine gun.

"They couldn't put Carmine's face back together again," Imperial growled at Vance. "And you think we should wait and ask them if they're cops or not, huh?"

"I didn't say that, Frank."

"Shut up, you moron! And do what I say. If they're cops they'll have papers. We'll know they're cops—"

"Frank! Look!" one of the men called urgently from a side window. "I see a car out there!"

138

"Where?" Frank Imperial rushed over to have a look for himself. When he saw the white Ford parked near the alley, he rapidly concluded, "They ain't cops! All right, you guys, take cover. That car tells me they ain't cops! Cops come in the front door!"

"Hey, Frank, they're here in front too," a second man called excitedly. "There's another car out here—and it looks like there's a guy sitting in it!"

"Is he wearing a uniform?" Imperial wanted to know.

"No—but wait a minute—now I see two more men coming around the car and, yes! They're in cop uniforms!"

"All I got to say," Imperial boomed, "is that if these guys were cops they would of come here in uniform—all of them!"

"That's right," Vance conceded. "You're right, Frank."

"They ain't no cops," Nicky concurred, shaking his head to show that he had no doubts.

"Hey, Frank! I see another one! A big guy—in the alley—behind that garbage can. He doesn't have no uniform on neither."

"Where?" Imperial wanted to see.

"Look, look, he's moving now, see?"

"Yeh."

Sliding tightly against the wall from behind one garbage can to another, Harry Calahan became, for an instant, clearly visible to the gangsters.

"That sure ain't no cop's gun," Frank Imperial said, noting Harry's .44 Magnum.

Suddenly there came a knock at the door. Each man aimed his gun there and looked to Imperial. Imperial raised three fingers of his right hand, indicating that he wanted the men to keep their trigger fingers relaxed for the moment.

The knock came again, this time more loudly.

Answering, Imperial yelled out, "We ain't open. Nobody's here. This is Sunday. Come back tomorrow."

"Police," one voice announced. "We'd like to ask you some questions."

"Open up," said a second voice. "Police."

"I'm just the watchman," Imperial growled. "There's nobody here. Come back tomorrow."

"Would you please open the door, sir," the first voice insisted, growing strained. "We're looking for Frank Imperial. We have a warrant here for his arrest."

Imperial motioned for the men to get ready to fire. He called out, "I told you that nobody's here!"

"We'll take a look anyway," the second voice called back. "We also have a warrant for a search of the premises. Now, for the last time, open up!"

"You got warrants," Imperial screamed, "then serve 'em!" He brought his hand down, cuing the others, and fired, blasting down the door.

Phil Sweet staggered back in a hail of bullets, clutching his heart. A look of horrified surprise froze in his eyes. He was hit again and again by the rain of bullets. The force of the blasts blew him backwards, causing him to twirl around and then drop to the ground, where he lay in a puddle of blood and shattered glass.

The volley of shots also reached Early Smith, who had been covering the two men from inside the car. At first he too was knocked back by the concussion, but he managed to pick himself up off the seat and scramble outside for cover. He ran around the car, pumping his shotgun as fast as he could into the building. Meanwhile, Davis was trapped in the crossfire, swearing furiously, crawling for refuge against an outside wall of the warehouse.

Early, reaching the opposite side of the car, opened the door and reached in for the radio.

"They got Sweet!" he yelled into the microphone. "They're chopping us up! Send units to help! Hurry! There must be a dozen of them in there!"

Meanwhile, Harry, caught totally unaware by the commotion, reacted fiercely, angry at himself for not having expected that the trouble might come so soon, and in such a deliberate manner. He shot up and opened rapid-fire into the warehouse. Just as he did so a window in the Buick shattered near his face. He twisted around and dropped for cover, moving closer to the building. Bullets drilled at him from all sides, one grazing the top of the car, another missing his head by less than an inch. A shotgun blast blew trash out of a nearby garbage can and all over him. An empty half-gallon milk container hit him in the face. Several strands of spaghetti caught his ear. He ducked lower and crawled behind the fallen can, bullets continuing to bounce everywhere around him. He got off two stray shots which ripped into the wood frame of the warehouse window.

His next shot, which penetrated the window, was followed by a crash and clatter from inside the warehouse. For a brief moment the firing ceased, allowing him the chance to roll up close to the building. He had just made it to the wall when suddenly a machine gun opened up, ripping through and tearing up the Buick.

Out front, Early continued firing as fast as he could pump the shotgun, and then, when that was emptied, he used his service pistol. He was breathing heavily.

Harry scrambled low along the outside warehouse wall until he came to the shattered window. He stabbed a quick look inside, spotting two men in another window still blasting at the trash can where they had last seen him.

In the far distance, the faint sound of approaching sirens could be heard.

Early, who was reloading the shotgun, let out a sigh of relief. Davis, meanwhile, was still pinned in the crossfire, still unable to get off a successful shot.

The man with the Thompson submachine gun spotted Harry's head retreating from the window and suddenly whipped around, plugging three holes into the wood under the windowsill, barely missing him. Harry's return fire caused the man to double over and fall backwards. A second man swung his gun to the window, shooting rapid-fire, but he could no longer see his target and the shots went wild.

Within moments squad cars, their sirens screaming, pulled up in the street. Their doors flung open and cops poured out on all sides, firing into the front of the warehouse with shotguns and service revolvers. Some of the cops stayed behind to cover the men who moved into attack position. After several explosive volleys, there came an instant of eerie silence when shooting ceased from within the warehouse.

A cop picked up a megaphone and commanded at the top of his voice, "Throw out your weapons and come out of there with your hands behind your heads. You have until I count to three. One . . ."

In the alley, Harry, crouched against the warehouse wall, gritted his teeth. He had his gun pointed on a side door when the door suddenly opened all the way and a man—it was Nicky—made a mad dash for the Buick.

"Two . . ." blared the cop out in front with the megaphone.

"Hold where you are!" Harry shouted at the fleeing man, catching him totally by surprise. The man reeled around, let off a fast shot, and then dove for the Buick. He managed to make it into the car, but then Harry shot him through the rear window before he could get it started. The man's head bounced forward from the blast, smacking the windshield before crashing down on the dashboard.

Harry plugged him one more time for good measure.

The cop with the megaphone, hearing the shots, stopped counting. The gunfight erupted again.

Suddenly a Cadillac bashed through a rear garage door directly in front of Harry. The car roared, coming straight at him. The driver was Frank Imperial.

Harry leveled the .44 with both hands and blasted. The bullet tore off a chrome strip at the edge of the windshield. Imperial swerved the car at him, ripping off more chrome as he scraped up against the warehouse wall. With no place else to go but the grave, Harry lunged for the hood of the car, almost smashing through the windshield as he did so.

Imperial stepped on the accelerator, brutally swiping the building and hurtling the Cadillac over an obstacle course of spilled garbage cans. The noise was deafening. Debris flew everywhere. One can came zinging by Harry's head. When he ducked to avoid it, another hit him full force, slashing his left cheek. He fought to stay conscious, leaning over to hold on to the windshield wipers. A piece of flying metal shattered the windshield only inches away from him.

He caught a brief look at Imperial's manic eyes. The gangster stood on the gas pedal, tearing the car through the alley toward the open street. Harry removed one hand from a wiper, and, as best he could, aimed his gun into the car. The shot sent an explosion of glass into Imperial's face. Harry followed with several more shots into the engine block.

There was a terrible screeching and grating sound as the bullets tore the engine block from its mounts and the drive train dislodged. The transmission went next, a split second later, and then the back end locked. Smoke poured out from under the hood. The car, completely out of control, ricocheted off the walls.

The wiper came off in Harry's hand. He slid down from the top of the car to the smoking hood before crashing to the ground, bloodied, bruised and very severely hurt in his left leg, chest and face.

Imperial broke from the Cadillac, dashing to the street. Harry, his eyelids half-shut from agony, saw the gangster making the break, rolled over, flinching from the pain, and whipped a fresh speedloader into the .44.

He yelled, "Halt!"

Imperial kept going. His gun loaded, Imperial just about to turn the corner into the street, Harry aimed and fired.

One shot did it.

Imperial went into a full flip and crashed head first into an oncoming milk truck. The driver of the truck, startled, stood on his brakes, but his reflexes were just a bit too slow. The tires screamed and the truck jackknifed, with Imperial glued to the grill, containers of milk spewing from the top and both sides of the truck. As each milk container hit the pavement, it burst open into a wet, white explosion. The street became a river of milk.

Finally, the truck careened into a parked car and came to a jarring stop.

Imperial fell off into a pool of milk, dead.

Harry collapsed against the smoking and wrecked Cadillac. Several cops ran toward him, Early in front.

Just before Harry lost consciousness he heard Early tell him, breath rasping in his lungs: "Sweet is dead! They got Sweet!"

Chapter 26

Harry Calahan, his leg and chest bandaged, sat up on the edge of a stainless steel bed in Mt. Zion Hospital. Jim Hamilton, a black doctor, was perched on a stool near the bed, washing a long gash on Harry's bruised forehead with an antiseptic solution. Hamilton, a good-natured fellow who was just beginning to get soured by his profession, had known Harry for five years. Needless to say, this was not the first time Dr. Hamilton found himself in a hospital room putting Dirty Harry back together again.

"Sure a nice job you did on yourself this time, Harry." Hamilton sighed, a mixture of compassion and admonition.

"Oooh! Be careful, doc, it hurts!" Harry flinched.

"It'll hurt a lot more—and a lot longer, Harry—if I don't get it clean. Sit still. They tell me you did a real job on Frank Imperial. I saw his body in the hallway."

"You mean that bastard's still alive?"

"No, I mean over at the morgue. He's about as dead as they ever get."

"Which still isn't dead enough." Harry sneered. "Will you hurry up? Jesus, that hurts, I said."

"About fifteen sutures now and we'll be all done," Hamilton said, reaching for an anesthetic. "I'll give you a local."

"Forget it."

"Are you kidding me, Harry?"

"No. I said no local. I don't like that stuff. Start sewing. Just get it over with."

"Okay," the doctor grimaced. "It's your ass, not mine."

"Head," Harry corrected him. "Head. Not my ass."

The doctor laughed through his nose and said, "Why does everybody suddenly become a comedian in here?"

"Maybe it's because you're such a funny sight to look at, doc."

Hamilton, smirking, threaded a surgical needle and went to work stitching up Harry's wound. Harry couldn't do much but squint his eyes and grind his teeth against the pull of the needle.

"Hold still," Hamilton told him.

Suddenly the door burst open and Briggs came charging in, nearly knocking down a nurse. The lieutenant was scowling and breathing heavily. Behind him, his superior, Captain Avery, also entered, wearing a look of torment on his face. He was dressed, as was Briggs, in a rumpled suit, with his tie pulled open at the collar.

Hamilton, trying to concentrate on the sutures, did not look up, but nonetheless let out a faint grunt. As well as his aching neck would allow, Harry turned and rolled up his eyes to greet the visitors. Both men stared him down icily, and then Briggs turned sharply to Hamilton.

"Does he have to stay here?" the lieutenant demanded of the doctor.

The doctor shot around. "No! Of course not! If you'd like I can let his brains run out all over your shoes. Just give the word, lieutenant."

Briggs shrank back, but Avery indicated that he did not appreciate the doctor's remark, and added, "Hamilton, I don't need to hear a doctor display that sort of attitude. A police officer is dead!"

"Sorry," Hamilton replied, meaning it.

Briggs then opened up on Harry. "I got warrants for a search of the premises, if I recall, Calahan. You were supposed to go in and take Imperial and that's all. A simple arrest! Nobody said for you to become judge, jury and executioner, goddamnit!"

Harry removed his eyes from the men and stared at the wall as the doctor continued the stitching. "Arresting a killer like Imperial isn't simple," he said.

"People are guilty until proven—" Briggs started shouting before he caught his error. "I mean people are— goddamnit, you know what I mean, Calahan. On top of everything else you're just plain dumb, that's all. Don't

146

you realize this city is on the edge of the worst criminal violence in its history. Jesus Christ! AND YOU GOTTA GO OUT THERE AND START FULL-SCALE MILITARY OPERATIONS!"

Harry replied almost in a whisper, "I didn't shoot anybody that wasn't trying to shoot me first, Briggs." His words were even and unemotional.

Avery erupted at Harry's couldn't-care-less tone. "Every time you pull that gun, Calahan, my paperwork backs up for the next three months. It's one mess after another with you. Do you realize that the chief has been calling me all day on this matter, Calahan? He told me to inform you that he's conducting a full investigation and that if you don't come up smelling like roses you're through! Finished, Calahan, and good riddance."

Harry, in the same near-whisper, his eyes still fixed on the wall, repeated, "I didn't shoot anybody that wasn't trying to shoot me first."

Avery did not want to hear. He gave Harry an extremely disgusted look, which Harry did not see, and stalked out. Briggs watched him leave and then turned around to shake an angry fist at Harry.

"What about a dead cop, Calahan?" he screamed. "I warned you against taking those rookies!"

"Sweet was killed with the first shot fired, Briggs. It was a set-up."

"A WHAT?"

"You heard me. They knew we were coming. Somebody tipped Imperial off."

"Don't hand me that shit, you liar. How?"

Hamilton finished the sutures, bandaged Harry's head, and got up to his feet, taking in a deep breath.

"After two hundred arrests, Briggs, I'm learning how to tell the difference." Harry turned full face on the lieutenant.

But Briggs was too upset to be rational. He hissed in a lowered voice, "If I have my way, Calahan, you won't make another arrest as long as you live!"

Harry did not appear to be in the least disturbed by the lieutenant's threat. He said, "Is that all?"

"No—that's not all! Give me that slug you showed me."

"What slug?"

"Don't play games with me, Calahan. Hand it over."

"Didn't turn out to be anything," Harry told him. "I checked it again with the lab. It was a different rifling twist, after all. You were right, Briggs."

Briggs shouted, "It's still state's evidence! Give it to me!"

"No."

"Then you're under arrest."

Harry shot him a drilling look and then reached over to a chair near the bed for his pants. He dug into a front pocket, retrieved the slug and then threw it at Briggs. It hit the lieutenant in the chest.

"Eat it," Harry said.

Briggs held himself on the edge of violence for a moment, clenched the slug in his hand and stormed out, slamming the door behind him.

The doctor shrugged and smiled at his patient. "Harry," he said sympathetically, "haven't you had enough yet?" The tone of this remark indicated that the doctor had asked himself the same question many times.

"Nothing else I know how to do," Harry replied candidly.

"I should have been a tailor," the doctor mused. "It's a lot quieter."

"Don't let it get you, doc."

"Sometimes it's hard not to let it get me."

"Why don't you quit? Go into private practice or something like that?"

"I don't know," Hamilton said. "I don't know. I think about it a lot. Maybe it's because my old man was a cop."

"I didn't know that," Harry said.

"He got plugged by some two-bit burglar when I was only twelve."

"That's too bad," Harry sympathized.

"Life." The doctor shook his head in resignation.

A nurse came to the door, announcing, "Doctor Hamilton, they need you urgently in surgery."

The doctor started out of the room, turning in the doorway.

"Sorry about all this, Harry," he said, then left.

Alone in the room, Harry sat up and squinted in the glare of the fluorescent lights. After a moment he hoisted himself off the bed. Stiffening under the pain, he began to get dressed.

Chapter 27

Early Smith waited in the hallway of the hospital. When the door to Room 504 opened and Harry, his bruised and bandaged partner, emerged, Smith went wide-eyed and did a double take.

"Christ," he said, shaking his head, "I hope you feel a whole lot better than you look."

"Let's get out of here," Harry said, not interested in hearing how he looked.

They took the elevator down to the street level and then walked to the parking lot behind the building. Neither man spoke again until they were in the car.

Early put the key in the ignition, took a deep breath, and said, "Look, Harry, I heard Briggs giving it to you. If it means anything, I think you got the wrong end of the stick."

"You do, eh?" Harry brightened, then winced suddenly. He was having problems getting comfortably situated in his seat.

Early started the car, checked the rear-view mirror and pulled out. At the first traffic light he turned to Harry and smiled sympathetically.

"What did they find out at Imperial's when they finally got in there?" Harry asked him, adjusting the bandage on his forehead.

"Nothing," Early replied. "That's the thing. Imperial was as clean as he could possibly be. I almost think he knew we were coming."

"Then why did they open up?" Harry tested.

"Maybe they thought it was a set-up, like all the others."

"It was," Harry said flatly.

To Early it had only been a theory. He was surprised to learn that Harry regarded it as something more substantial. "What are you trying to say?" he wanted to know.

Harry came directly to the point. "Somebody tipped them off that we were coming."

"No!" Early couldn't believe it.

"Yes," Harry said wearily. "Sorry to say, but I'm not joking. It's so farfetched I can hardly believe it myself."

Early flashed a nervous grin, then resigned himself. "I think I'll give up being surprised anymore, working with you."

"You will, huh?" Harry said. "Well, try this on for size: The guys responsible for knocking off every slimy character in town—as well as one not so slimy character, my friend Charlie McCoy—are a bunch of rookie cops."

Early pulled to the curb, jamming on the brakes. It was with a fallen jaw that he watched Harry reach into a pocket and hand him a slug.

Early's eyes became question marks as he examined it.

"That," Harry explained, "is a slug I pulled from the target range. It comes from Davis's Smith and Wesson. It matches—exactly—the ones we found in Charlie McCoy's skull."

"Davis!" Early was shocked. "Harry, that's insane, considering—"

"Let me make the point clearly, Smith. Davis and those buddies of his are responsible for all these killings. That bullet you have in your hands proves it."

Early shook his head in utter disbelief.

"But that's insane," he insisted. "Absolutely insane!"

"Wrong. These guys think they're very sane. They figure that since the law's doing so little these days to take care of criminals, they got a right to do it themselves. It's a moral thing with them. That's my guess."

"I saw Briggs come out of your room with another slug in his hand, Harry. What was that?"

"A phony."

"I don't get it."

"The other day I took him to the lab and showed him the bullets back to back, but he wouldn't believe his own eyes. Tried to tell me that they didn't match up enough to make a case in court."

"Did you tell him where it came from?"

"No, I didn't. And as a matter of fact when he asked —rather, demanded—that I turn the slug over to him a few minutes ago, he didn't even ask where it had come from."

"He was pretty riled up, Harry. Not too rational. Avery was all over him."

"Maybe. But the facts of the case are this: There's no doubt whatsoever that it matches the bullet which killed Charlie McCoy and there's a damn good chance—even though I haven't been able to prove it yet—that it might also match the slugs they took out of Bubby Ricca. And secondly, it was either Davis or Sweet or Grimes or Astrachan who tipped off Imperial that we were coming. Either way, they must have figured it would work out fine for them, that I'd get knocked off or Imperial'd get knocked off, and hopefully both."

"Harry—but Sweet died this morning!"

"He was sacrificed."

"Jesus."

"But what's more important, Early, is that if I'm right I'll also be sacrificed. And then they've got to figure that I told you, so you're likely to be sacrificed too. Do you follow me?"

"I'm afraid I do. Loud and clear. But, I mean, it's all just too much."

"If I get sacrificed first I want you to take that bullet to Briggs. No, better yet, to Avery."

"What happens if they get both of us?" Early slid forward in his seat.

"Then they win."

Early flopped back and shut his eyes. His face filled with exasperation.

"Now how about getting this car moving again?" Harry said. "Drop yourself off first. I'll take the car home with me and pick you up in the morning."

Early collected himself and put the car back in gear. As they drove along through a decaying neighborhood of mostly one-family homes, Harry became philosophical.

"Maybe they're right in some ways," he mused. "It's not

152

hard to understand. It's rotten—but it's not hard to understand. Who knows how big it is? I know it sounds impossible, but there could very well be a whole suborganization within the force. A similar thing happened in Brazil a few years back."

"Wow! It didn't occur to me that it could be that big! I guess we come from a different world, Harry."

"Yeh," Harry sighed. "Sometimes at about two o'clock in the morning I wonder where in the hell that world went to."

Early pulled into a high-rise housing development and stopped the car at the entrance to one of the buildings. Leading up into the building was a maze of wooden catwalks, draining ditches, sewer pipes and gas lines. The development was still under construction, although many families, like the Smiths, had already moved in.

Early got out of the car and Harry came around to the driver's side.

"I hope to see you later," Harry said, tapping his partner affectionately on the shoulder as he passed.

Suddenly, from behind them, an ear-shattering blast erupted. They whipped around at the sound, reaching for their guns.

Early was first to see what it was. "It's just a coal truck making a delivery," he said, wiping his brow.

Harry angrily holstered his gun. He was irritated. "Who the hell still uses coal?" he asked.

"Not too many people," Early said, patting him on the shoulder. "People are using it less and less. Did I ever tell you that my old man once drove a coal truck? He went up north for a couple of years, to make some money, and that was the last we saw of him. One day he put his head down on the bed of his truck and the dumper came down on him. We had to keep the box closed at his funeral. They put his picture on top of the box. That was the last I saw of him—that picture."

"That's too bad," Harry sympathized.

"Hey, look, Harry. Why don't you come up and join us for dinner?"

Harry shook his head negatively. "Not tonight, Early. I got some things I want to take care of."

"Sure?"

"Yeh." He shook Early's hand warmly. "Later," he said.

"I certainly hope so." Early tried to laugh.

"I'll take a raincheck on that sit-down dinner, if you don't mind."

"Any time, Harry. Any time."

Harry's face creased in a grin. Early waved and started up the crosswalk. Harry got behind the wheel, swung the car around in a U-turn and started home.

Early stopped, turned around, and watched the car disappearing. Then, instead of heading up to his apartment, he decided to run over to a supermarket across the street to buy a watermelon for dessert.

Chapter 28

As Harry Calahan pulled into the parking lot of his own apartment building he saw his acquaintance from several nights back, the young, stunning, long-haired Oriental girl who lived on the first floor, roaring out in a small beat-up foreign convertible, hair whipping across her face. Spotting Harry, she braked the car and smiled from ear to ear. Harry pretended not to notice her and drove by.

"Hey!" she called, turning around.

Harry hit his brakes and backed up alongside her car, smiling reluctantly.

"Hi," the girl said. Then she got a better look at him. "Jesus, Harry, what happened to you?"

"Nothing," Harry replied with his usual understatement. "Just a few stitches."

She paused, contemplating the injuries. After a moment she said, "I was just going to the market. I'll tell you what—I could bring some beer back, if you like."

Against his better judgment, Harry could not prevent himself from saying, "You know, I could go for a few beers right now."

"Okay," she brightened. "I'll be right back. Why don't you just go right up to your place? I still have your spare key, so I'll even check your mail for you."

Harry nodded and grinned. "Okay."

"Keep it warm," the girl said, then winked.

Harry grinned.

The girl laughed and then left him with a jaunty wave as she squealed out of the parking lot. In spite of his other preoccupations, Harry couldn't help feeling lifted. He pulled the car into the spot marked "Calahan," shut

155

off the ignition, pocketed the keys and started up from the underground garage to the building.

Suddenly, from behind, he heard a familiar voice address him sharply.

It said, "Do you have any idea how hard it is to prosecute a cop?"

Harry turned on his heels and saw Davis, Grimes and Astrachan walking out from between two parked cars. Their motorcycles were parked a few feet away.

The voice belonged to Davis, who stared at Harry for a long uncomfortable moment and then repeated himself, more to the point, "Do you have any *idea* how hard it would be to prosecute us?"

Harry straightened up and sneered. "You heroes killed a dozen men last week. What are you figuring on doing next week?"

Davis replied flatly, "Maybe kill another dozen."

"So that's what you guys are all about, huh? Being heroes?" Harry tightened his jaw.

Astrachan fielded the question, replying, without a trace of humor, "All our heroes are dead."

"Ha, ha, Astrachan. Very funny," Harry replied facetiously.

"We're the first generation on the force that knows how to fight," Davis said, righteously jutting his chest forward. He and the others were all dressed in their uniforms. "We're only ridding society of killers that would be caught and executed anyway if the courts worked the way they're supposed to work. We've started with criminals like Ricca and Guzman, the big shots, so that the people will understand our action. There's enough of a criminal element in this town to keep us busy for a long time to come. We can't tolerate any interference. It's not just a question whether to use violence or not, either. There's just no other way, Harry."

"*Inspector* Calahan to you, Davis."

"You of all people should understand that."

Davis's point struck a deep sympathetic chord in Harry. There was a long moment of crackling silence when he said nothing and looked Davis straight in the eye.

It was Grimes who precipitously broke the silence. "You're either for us or against us," he demanded. "There can be no in-between."

Harry turned his head sharply to face Grimes when he replied coldly, "I'm afraid you misjudged me, punk."

"We're sorry to hear that, Harry," Davis spoke up. "Very sorry." He turned to motion Grimes and Astrachan and then said, "Let's go, fellas."

The three patrolmen stalked to their motorcycles, started up, shot Harry ominous looks, and then roared off. Harry stood in place for a moment, watching them leave, motionless, drawing in a deep breath of air. His face showed only exhaustion.

He continued into the vestibule of the building, where he stopped automatically at his mailbox, fumbling for the key. Then, on second thought, he decided against using the key. Instead, he stuck the stub of a pencil into the mailbox. However, something on the inside prevented the pencil from going all the way through. He withdrew the pencil, bit his lip, raised his eyes and shook his head. Grimacing, he put the pencil back into his pocket, and without opening the mailbox unlocked an inner glass door to the lobby and went up the steps to his apartment, quickly and noiselessly.

He was careful not to stand directly in front of the apartment door, and only after first listening carefully for any sound from the inside did he unlock it, allowing it to swing open by itself. He stood off to one side, gun drawn. When nothing in the apartment stirred, he peeked in. It seemed to be empty. He walked in, looking quickly in all directions, then holstered the gun.

Suddenly, with the door still open, the light bulb in the hallway flickered out. Harry heard a shuffle and ran to the door, drawing the gun again. In the dense quiet, he heard footsteps.

He shot a glance into the darkened hallway, where he continued to hear the shuffle of footsteps. He looked up and down the corridor, but was unable to see anything.

The footsteps grew louder. Finally a thin figure became visible, passing the opened door.

It was an old lady pulling a shopping cart full of laundry, staring straight ahead. She failed to notice Harry aiming the .44 directly at her head.

Harry held the gun on the old lady until she disappeared from sight, then he walked back into the apartment and shut the door. He took off his jacket, tossing it on the couch, and after stopping in the bathroom to relieve himself went to the refrigerator for a snack and a beer. He found a leftover hamburger to snack on, but no beer. The thought of the beer made him suddenly remember that the Oriental girl had said she would check his mail.

"Christ," he said aloud. He bolted out the door and down the steps, banging against the railing. He tore down three steps at a time, out of breath, hurting all over.

"Christ," he said again, angry at himself for not having remembered sooner.

At the bottom of the steps he streaked through the lobby.

In the vestibule, the girl was already back, toting two bags of groceries and a six pack of beer. She came up to the mailboxes and braced the bags against the wall with one knee under them. She reached into her purse for her keys and just as she was about to insert one into the mailbox marked "Calahan," Harry came through the door, yelling "Stop!" He dove at her, knocking her ass—backwards, causing groceries and beer cans to fly out of the bags.

The girl lay sprawled and dazed on the floor, unable to say a thing. All the wind had been knocked out of her.

Harry did not even bother to waste time apologizing. He pulled out a pocket knife and used it to unscrew a plate that covered all the mailboxes and buzzers. He worked very carefully, cautious not to jolt anything or allow any part to slip from his hands.

The girl began coming back to herself, trying to sit up.

A heavyset man appeared from the doorway of an apartment that opened up into the lobby. He wore an undershirt and a suspicious face. After a moment of peering at Harry through the glass door, he spotted the girl on the floor and stalked into the vestibule.

Without removing his hands from the mailbox, Harry glanced over his shoulder to see who it was.

"Hey," the man demanded, "what's going on here?"

"I'm taking this apart." Harry was irritated by the man's intrusion. "What's it look like?"

The man sized him up. "You live here, don't you?" His tone suggested that he wasn't clear whether or not Harry did.

"Yeh," Harry replied curtly. He remained all concentration on the mailboxes.

The man was not yet satisfied. "Well then, what in the hell are you doing to those mailboxes? Did you lose your key or something?"

Harry did not appreciate his tone. "Mind your own goddamn business," he said sharply without turning around.

"That happens to be my mailbox too, mister; so don't get smart with me." The man moved closer.

Harry shot him an extremely nasty look, but otherwise continued to ignore him. He took the last few screws out and pulled the face plate away from the wall. He dropped the screws into a pocket, and, holding the plate with one hand, began feeling inside with the other.

The girl, staring at him with large, curious eyes, did not say a thing. Harry pulled a small metal part out of the mailbox and threw it to the floor.

The man grew angry and announced, "Tampering with the mails is a federal offense."

"Is that so?" Harry sneered without turning around.

"Okay, buddy, I'm calling the police."

"I am the police," Harry said tightly, deliberately pausing between each word.

The man's jaw fell in disbelief. "What? You mean you're the cop that lives upstairs?" There was a new, conciliatory note in his voice.

"That's right," Harry told him. "Now shut up." He rested the plate on the floor and then reached for a gob of plastic material in his mailbox. The device was wrapped in wires, one of which led to the keyhole. Harry disconnected it.

"What's that?" the man asked nervously.

Harry checked to be sure he had it thoroughly disconnected, then took the device out of the mailbox, turning to face the man. He said, without emotion, "It's a plastic explosive."

"A bomb!" The man was horrified. He backed up rapidly, reaching for the door handle.

"If you'd bothered me just a little bit more," Harry shouted to him, "there's a good chance that we'd all be stuck to the wall now."

"I don't want to be involved." The man backed off, all jitters. He opened the door and slipped through, slamming it behind him.

Harry turned to the girl, who was still on the floor, staring at the gaping hole in the wall. Her face was full of fear and wonder. Harry saw her shaking.

He extended her a hand, helping her up.

"Christ," was all she could say.

"Go to your apartment," Harry said. "Stay there all night. Lock the door and don't open it for anyone but me. Not anyone. Do you understand?"

She nodded yes and wobbled back to her apartment, trembling all the way.

Chapter 29

Once he got to the supermarket, Early Smith decided to pick up a few items in addition to the watermelon. He filled a basket with pretzels, celery, cashew nuts, cheese and a half–gallon of California burgundy. But then at the check-out counter he found himself without enough cash to pay.

"I'll have to write a check," he told the cashier.

"Do you have a check-cashing card, sir?"

"No, but—"

"Then you'll have to have your check approved by the manager. He's over there." She pointed over her shoulder to an elevated glass-enclosed booth where the manager was sitting behind a desk, watching over the twelve check-out counters.

Early looked up at the man. Just as he did, the manager caught his eye and waved enthusiastically. Early waved back, smiling. The cashier saw the exchange and said, "I guess that won't be necessary, sir. How much would you like to write the check for?"

"How about twenty?"

"Fine."

The groceries fit into two bags. Early took one in each hand and started across the street. He made it halfway and then got stranded for a few moments on a concrete island. He stepped into the crosswalk and several cars stopped for him as he continued to the other side.

He walked to the maze of boardwalks that led into his apartment building.

"Howdy, Inspector."

Early looked up and saw a friendly, familiar male face passing, but he could not remember the man's name. He said, "Hi, there."

"Nice weather we're having," the man said.

"Isn't it?" Early replied.

"Say," the man said, raising a hand, "from the papers, it looks like you fellas in the police department sure have your hands full these days."

"Yeh," Early grinned, flexing the bags, "we sure do."

"Well," the man smiled, continuing, "I want you to know it's sure nice to have men like you there working for us. And lots of people feel the same way I do."

"Thanks," Early said. He took a few steps more and pulled a piece of celery from one of the bags, then chomped on it as he walked.

When he reached the apartment building, he wedged a bag up against the door and opened it. In the lobby, an elderly black couple nodded to him. The woman said, "Hello, Inspector, how are you today?"

Early smiled and said, "Fine."

He turned the corner, shifting the bags in his arms. When he got to the mailboxes he put the groceries down and searched a pocket for his keys.

He found the correct key and inserted it into the lock. It was the last thing he ever did.

There was a blinding flash and a tremendous, ear-shattering explosion. Detective Early Smith became, for an instant, a red blur in a terrible burst of concrete, steel and glass.

Then he spun to the floor; dead, with a half-eaten stalk of celery still in his hand.

Chapter 30

Harry Calahan brought the plastic explosive up to his apartment and placed it on top of the television set. After inspecting it carefully for a few moments he went to the telephone and dialed a number. He let it ring for almost a minute, but there was no answer. Swearing angrily, he hung up and tried a second number. A female voice answered, "Police Department, may I help you?"

"Homicide—Detective Lieutenant Briggs," Harry said. "Inspector Calahan calling. It's urgent."

The switchboard operator interrupted Briggs, who was on another call, and put Harry through.

"Calahan!" Briggs said, a little surprised. "Where are you?"

Harry flinched at the question. Then he said, "Briggs, I just found a bomb in my mailbox. Get a man over to Early's right away. There's probably one in his mailbox, too."

"What?" Briggs bellowed.

"I've got it right here in my hand, Briggs. It's completely disarmed. Now get a man over to Early's—and quick!"

"I'll get right on it," Briggs said excitedly. "You stay right where you are! I'll be down there myself! Listen to me now, don't move!" He hung up abruptly.

Harry put down the dead receiver and went into his bedroom. He opened the top drawer of his dresser and reached in to get a switch-blade stiletto. He snapped open the blade to check it, then closed the knife and pushed it down to rest against the small of his back, under his belt.

Next he checked his .44 Magnum and placed three

speedloaders in his pocket. Then he went back to the living room and sat down in a chair facing the door.

Fifteen minutes later somebody knocked. Harry aimed the gun at the door.

"Who is it?" he demanded.

"Harry?"

"I said *who is it!*"

"It's Briggs. Are you all right? Open up."

"Come on in. It's open."

The door swung open. Briggs took a few steps and flinched at the sight of the .44. Harry looked from Briggs to the gun, and then holstered it after an uncomfortable pause.

"I don't like looking down one of those," Briggs said, not too lightly.

"Did anybody see you out there?" Harry asked, getting up.

"No, not that I know of."

Harry walked to the window and looked down to the street. "I don't see any squad cars out there."

"I came alone," Briggs replied. "Where's the bomb?"

"Right over there." Harry pointed to the television set. Briggs walked over and picked it up, inspecting it closely. In a moment he stuck it in the pocket of his jacket and turned around.

"All right, Harry," he said. "Let's get out of here. Avery is waiting to see us."

Harry extended his arm, motioning for Briggs to leave first. He followed after him, locking the door.

Briggs had parked his car in front, leaving the motor running. Inside, the radio crackled. Briggs started for the driver's side, then stopped and asked, "You in any condition to drive, Harry?"

"Why?" Harry measured him.

"I'd like to take a closer look at this thing," he said, digging into his pocket for the bomb.

Harry nodded, walked around the car, slid in behind the wheel, put the car in gear and pulled out.

He drove a few blocks in silence while Briggs again examined the plastic explosive. Finally Briggs put it down on the seat and said, "This thing could have been activated by your mailbox key, or if somebody wanted they could've also rigged it with the timer."

Harry reached a stop light. He turned his head and regarded the lieutenant with unrelenting eyes.

Two hundred yards behind the car a police motorcycle emerged from an alley and began following them.

Suddenly Briggs said loudly, "Get on the freeway, Calahan."

"You got a new route to headquarters?" Harry asked sarcastically.

"Do as I say!" Briggs whipped out a .45 automatic and jabbed it at Harry's neck.

Harry did not appear to be all that surprised. Remaining cool, he said, "Your gun is out of the holster, Briggs. Is this the first time?"

"Shut up!"

"Or what is that you once told me, Briggs? That the best guns always stay in their holsters?"

"I said shut up and drive, Calahan!"

"What's this all about, Briggs?"

"You're not going to headquarters, Calahan. The only way you're going anywhere is in a rubber bag."

Briggs steadied his .45 at Harry's skull and removed the Magnum from Harry's holster.

"Now hand over the shells," he commanded.

As he continued driving, Harry took two speedloaders out of his pocket and tossed them over.

"Three!" Briggs demanded. "You always carry three!"

Harry threw him the third one.

Briggs rolled down the window with his free hand and tossed out the three speedloaders. They bounced off the pavement of the on-ramp to the freeway.

The motorcycle continued to follow at a steady distance behind their car. However, Harry, unlike Briggs, still failed to distinguish it from the tangle of traffic filling his rear-view mirror.

"I'd like to know how you expect to cover this one," Harry asked reasonably.

"I run the investigation, Calahan, and with your record I could make anything stick!"

Harry glanced over at the lieutenant and said, "Why are you doing this, Briggs? You, of all people?"

"You shouldn't find it so strange, Calahan. A hundred years ago in this city people did the exact same thing, more or less. History justified the vigilantes. We're no different. The legal process has broken down and somebody has to protect society. It's as simple as that. Anyone who threatens the safety of the people will be executed. Evil for evil, Harry. Retribution!"

"I believe in that, Briggs," Harry said, his eyes on the road, "but I don't believe in murder. Once the police become their own executioners, where will it stop? Who says you won't be executing people for jaywalking? Even for traffic tickets? Or maybe you'll figure you got the right to kill your next-door neighbor because his dog pissed on your lawn!"

"There isn't one man we killed that didn't get precisely what was coming to him."

"Wrong, Briggs! There was—one. And he happened to be my pal, Charlie McCoy."

"What would you have done, Harry?" Briggs asked after a pensive pause.

"I would have upheld the law."

Briggs glanced quickly into the rear-view mirror, checking on the motorcycle, which continued to follow. Then, fully digesting what Harry said, he replied passionately, "Bullshit! What the hell do you know about the law, Calahan! You're a great cop, I'll admit, but you're not a team player. You had your chance, Harry, a little while ago—to join the team—but you made it very clear that you'd rather stick with the system."

"Briggs—I hate the damn system, but it happens to be the only one we got. And one thing I like about it is that it doesn't include murder. Now, until that's changed, I intend to go along with it."

"I'm genuinely sorry to hear you say that, Harry. Somehow I thought you'd see the point."

"Briggs, you make about as much sense as tits on a bull."

"Wrong, Calahan! You're about to see just how much sense I really make! Because you're about to become extinct!" The bile rose in Briggs's throat as he drew his face back fiercely, preparing to fire.

Harry stabbed the brakes, cutting hard, and at the same time holding the accelerator to the floor. Briggs's shot went stray, grazing Harry's neck and shattering his window. Briggs was slammed up against the dashboard. He dropped the gun.

The tires screeched horribly and the car, weaving in and out, missed several others by an eyeblink. Horns began to blare. Three cars in the middle lane crashed into one another. Still driving, Harry freed a hand from the wheel and, as Briggs began to recover, chopped him viciously on the bridge of the nose.

Briggs was stunned by the pain, and fell back against the seat. Harry grabbed a handful of the lieutenant's hair and banged his head full force into the radio. Briggs drooped over and fell to the floor.

* * *

Chapter 31

A sudden wrenching shock shuddered through the car as it careened off a lightpole and spun backwards into an exit ramp, plumes of smoke spewing from the tires. Briggs lay unconscious by the glove compartment. Harry, his face taut with pain—his neck bleeding where the bullet had grazed it—wheeled the car around and barreled down the exit ramp.

In the rear-view mirror he noticed, for the first time, the motorcycle. It had separated from the confusion on the freeway and was following him several hundred yards behind. He squinted hard to see who it was, but was unable to make out the man's face.

Leaving the exit ramp, Harry turned the car sharply onto a secondary road, driving fast. For the first mile or two the motorcycle held a steady distance, but then when traffic suddenly died in the oncoming lane it veered to the left and began closing in.

At that instant Harry was finally able to get a good look at his pursuer's face. It was Grimes.

Grimes continued to pick up speed on the motorcycle and closed to within a car's length of Harry. He drew his gun, leveled it, and fired.

The shot blasted through the rear window of the car and hit the rear-view mirror, shattering it. As Harry ducked to avoid the flying fragments of glass, his car momentarily slid, out of control, onto a dirt shoulder. He regained a solid hold on the wheel and veered the car back to the road. A sign reading "Suisun Bay" loomed ahead and whipped by.

Up ahead a short distance he saw a drawbridge, and an oil tanker approaching in the channel.

In trying for a second shot, Grimes lost his balance and

the motorcycle hit the shoulder in a screaming, dust-churning slide. He recovered quickly, set the machine back on the road and continued to tear after Harry.

Certain that the drawbridge would rise at any moment to accommodate the tanker, Harry stood hard on the brakes, burning whatever was left of the tires. But it was too late. With lights flashing on both sides, the bridge began to lift against the sky.

Since he was already at the bridge—still doing at least forty miles per hour—Harry was left with no choice but to give up on the brakes. He kicked his foot into the accelerator and the car roared up, sailing through the air like a strange flying machine before plunging down on the other side of the bridge. It came down so hard that the rocker panels caved in. The bottom of the car scraped violently against the steel-webbed siding of the bridge, and as the car slid back down to the road Harry was slammed against the roof.

His hands snapped from the wheel. The car pitched forward, smashing into a lightpole. Briggs, still unconscious, was thrown back up on the seat. The bomb slammed against the windshield, but fortunately did not explode.

Harry, although suffering from bruises and injuries all over his body, recovered and regained control of the wheel. The car screeched as he backed it up from the lightpole at the same moment that Grimes powered the motorcycle up the bridge, sailing over the water in a stupendous arc.

The motorcycle came down on its rear wheel, bouncing several times. As the motorcycle rolled down the bridge, Harry squealed the car around and slammed down on the gas pedal. He smashed head-on into the motorcycle, causing it to flip over the car's roof and detonate into a fireball as it crashed to the pavement. Grimes was thrown several hundred feet into a chaparral-covered field.

In the distance, Harry heard the roar of other motorcycles approaching, and then saw them—there were two—cornering rapidly from an intersecting road.

He wheeled the car around again, inadvertently demolishing a roadside sign that read: NAVAL RESERVE

DEFENSE FLEET—M.A.R.A.D. He continued up the road a few hundred feet and turned through a gate into the former naval base.

The two motorcycles followed, gaining on him.

The paved road turned to dirt as Harry proceeded into the deserted base and came up to a gray purgatory of obsolete warships—the mothball fleet—moored in neat rows, their huge silhouettes looming up in the sunset. Aluminum bubbles covered the artillery on each ship.

He screeched the car to a halt near a wooden gangway. He lurched out of the car, tearing for the gangway, and scrambled up the steep wood incline toward an attack carrier. Short of breath, his face severely bruised, blood streaming down his neck, he faltered somewhat and then, at the top of the gangway, collapsed to his knees. He pulled himself up, turning to watch as the motorcycles whipped through the gate, throwing up dust on all sides. Squinting, Harry recognized that the men were—as he fully expected —the two remaining musketeers, Davis and Astrachan.

He turned back and staggered onto the awesome flight deck of the attack carrier. Davis and Astrachan, approaching fast, got off several shots, their bullets cracking through the air and whining off the steel deck.

Severely out of breath, he somehow managed to gather one more incredible spurt of energy, tapping it to lunge across the deck toward the ship's command superstructure.

Davis and Astrachan roared their motorcycles onto the rickety ramps, tearing boards loose as they came sailing through the air, landing on the very edge of the carrier's deck.

Harry darted through a hatchway to the superstructure.

Astrachan skidded to a stop and dismounted. Unlimbering a folding stock Thompson, he took off for the nearest hatch. Davis, meanwhile, sped his motorcycle to the far end of the deck, where he broke to a sliding stop. Vaulting off the machine, he whipped out his long-barreled .357 Magnum and raced to a hatch.

As he came up on the hatch, Davis kept low and flat against the wall, pumping a full clip inside. Flame came spitting from the barrel of his gun and the whizzing bullets reverberated off various steel objects in a series of pings. When he finished shooting, there was a brief hiatus of absolute silence.

Harry crouched against the bulkhead, trying to catch his breath. Spotting him, Astrachan opened fire. Harry sought and quickly found cover behind an open door in the narrow corridor, but he was still endangered by the bullets ricocheting off the steel walls. One missed his nose by less than an inch. He rolled from the gunfire, groping for a nearby stairway. He painfully climbed the steps.

Astrachan momentarily lost him, but then Davis suddenly appeared at the foot of the stairway, unloading a second clip in a barrage that left the steel steps vibrating. The bullets whistled around Harry's legs. He pitched, hit the landing and rolled onto an overhead catwalk. Davis emptied the clip, opened the cylinder and jammed in a speedloader.

When Astrachan came rushing down the corridor, he looked up and spotted Harry scrambling overhead on the catwalk. But it was only for a split instant that he held Harry's figure in his eyes. By the time he pulled the trigger, Harry was again out of sight.

Davis couldn't see him either, and had to rely on the sound of Harry's footsteps to unload his next clip. His ears proved almost deadly accurate. Several shots clanged around Harry and barely missed him. He clambered onto another section of the catwalk as Astrachan, followed by Davis, stalked up the steps after him.

The shooting stopped for a few moments while the chase ensued. Then, suddenly, in a flash, Davis caught a glimpse of Harry coming out of the shadows. He aimed and squeezed the trigger.

Harry abruptly dropped from sight. Davis heard a heavy thud hit the floor, followed by another moment of absolute stillness.

"Red! Watch out!" Davis yelled at the top of his lungs. "I think he's coming your way."

Astrachan froze for a cataleptic second, waiting. Suddenly the metal catwalk began resounding with the high-pitched ring of scrambling footsteps. Astrachan raised his gun and fired a sustained burst at the sound. The shots echoed three and four times over, creating the audio illusion of an entire artillery squad popping off at once.

In another instant Davis caught a glimpse of Harry running across the catwalk. To Astrachan, he looked like a moving series of brilliant heat flashes.

As soon as he was behind cover again, Harry pulled out his knife and snapped it open.

Again, there was a brief intermission of echoing stillness.

Astrachan whipped a fresh clip into the Thompson.

"Red?" Davis called out. It echoed.

"He's not returning fire! Nothing!" Astrachan shouted back. "I don't think he has a gun. I think we have him."

At that moment Harry came up from behind and grabbed Astrachan by the neck. He squeezed, locked, and lunged the knife in. Astrachan dropped the Thompson, croaking out an eerie cry from his throat. He staggered forward in the shadows, clutching his bloody neck. Astrachan's cry ended with a gurgle and a choke. He fell over face first.

"Red?" Davis shouted. "Red? Are you all right?"

There was only silence.

Then Harry: "Briggs was right, Davis. You guys need more experience."

Taking Astrachan had cost Harry terribly. His wounds were a mess; blood dribbled over his lips, and it was only with great effort that he was able to keep his left eye open.

He stopped where he was for a moment, trying valiantly to keep his breath from croaking too loudly. It was a losing battle. Davis could easily hear the sound of the injured breathing, and he edged along the catwalk, closing in. He saw Harry through a shaft of light and whipped up his gun to shoot. The bullet pinged the steel and ricocheted. He squeezed off another shot, then snapped open the empty cylinder, throwing the Magnum down in disgust.

Harry heard the gun clatter on the steel floor.

"Now, what you're probably thinking, Davis," Harry called out from somewhere in the shadows, "is: Does he have a gun or not? But it really doesn't matter to me, Davis, because I have it in my mind to beat you to death anyway. So what you gotta ask yourself is: Are you feeling brave, punk?"

Davis was about to reply that he was feeling very brave when he cocked his head, hearing a familiar high-pitched wailing in the distance—sirens. After a moment's hesitation, he vaulted his cover and scrambled toward the hatch. He ran furiously and recklessly, slamming into the wall and several posts.

Harry started for the exit closest to him. Plunging through the hatchway, he saw Astrachan's motorcycle parked on the flight deck. The sound of the sirens grew nearer.

Summoning all his energy, Harry dashed across the deck, straining, scrambling for the motorcycle. As he mounted, he saw Davis darting out of another hatch.

Harry mounted the motorcycle, kicking once, twice, three times before it finally roared up. He wheeled out, tearing across the deck toward Davis, opening the throttle fully, flying and half skidding, peeling rubber.

Davis lunged for his motorcycle and tried frantically to get the machine started. He succeeded only when Harry was almost on top of him. Rearing up on one wheel, Davis powered out, smoking rubber in Harry's face. He turned for dockside, closing dangerously with the far end of the deck.

Harry lay his machine down at near eighty, standing up at one side.

Davis's motorcycle screeched and slid across the deck of the carrier, scraping the steel railing. The steel bike against steel railing created a tremendous burst of sparks. Davis suddenly disappeared in a blaze of shuddering light.

At the last possible instant Harry jumped from his machine and sent it crashing into Davis's blazing motorcycle. It hit with an enormous concussive force. Davis back-flipped into mid-air, soaring over the bay. The motorcycles tangled together and flew off after him, plunging down and hitting the bay with an impact violent enough to send water splashing all the way back up to the deck.

After pitching off his motorcycle, Harry rolled over several times. When he came to a stop, he found himself only a few feet from the edge. For a moment he lay there, catching his breath.

Stumbling at first, he wrenched himself up off the deck, grimacing as he looked down at his mess of wounds. A fierce wind blowing across the carrier almost toppled him before he managed to steady his balance. He walked a few steps to where he saw Davis's helmet, and kicked it over the edge. He continued to stare at the helmet until it dwindled to just a white speck in the dusk, disappearing into nothingness after it hit the dark water. Harry turned around, measured his breathing, then made his way, as best as he could, back down the gangway to the car.

He pulled open the car door and staggered in, reaching for his keys.

"Hold it right where you are, Calahan!"

Briggs shot up off the seat, leveling a gun at Harry's head. The lieutenant's swollen face was caked with dried blood. He looked like he was doing all he could to keep from passing out.

Harry flinched back spastically.

"No tricks, Calahan!" Briggs lowered the gun and jabbed it into Harry's ribs. Harry doubled over at the wheel, grunting. It took him a moment to recover, and when he did he raised his eyes and steadied them on Briggs.

"Briggs, your organization is all through," he said. As he spoke, his right hand, unseen to Briggs, groped along the seat, feeling for the bomb.

"I'll train more," Briggs boomed. "Don't worry, Calahan, there's lots more where those guys came from. Now get out of the car."

Harry drilled him in the eyes until he found the bomb with his hand. He pressed a switch to activate the timing mechanism. Then he slid out, slamming the door behind him.

Briggs aimed the gun on him through the window. "Uphold the law," he laughed. "Calahan, you hypocrite, you just killed two police officers! Or is it three? I should

174

shoot you right now. In fact, the only reason I'm not going to is that I'd rather prosecute you. Ha, ha, Calahan. I'm going to prosecute you with your own great system. Eat that! You don't have a chance! Because what it's all about, Calahan, is my word against yours. And with your reputation, who's going to believe you? Nobody! That's who. You're a killer, Calahan, a maniac."

"That's generous of you, Briggs, but what would you call yourself?"

"A hero, Calahan. A hero."

Saying that, Briggs swung his chin forward, fired the ignition, and jammed the car into gear, powering out in a wide, screeching turn. Harry turned and watched him drive off down the dirt road. He did not blink until a few moments later, when the car instantly exploded into a million fiery fragments.

Harry was still staring at the flames when the squad cars arrived, their sirens howling and red lights pulsating. All at once a dozen doors swung open and a charge of uniforms rushed toward him. At the head of the pack was Captain Avery.

"What the hell is going on here, Calahan?" he shouted. "What happened to you?"

"I never used my gun once," Harry replied quietly. He looked up one more time at Briggs's pyre, then turned and staggered to the comfort of the nearest squad car, his silhouette a small moving blur.

Wyndham Books are obtainable from many booksellers and newsagents. If you have any difficulty please send purchase price plus postage on the scale below to:

Wyndham Cash Sales
P.O. Box 11
Falmouth
Cornwall
OR
Star Book Service,
G.P.O. Box 29,
Douglas,
Isle of Man,
British Isles.

While every effort is made to keep prices low, it is sometimes necessary to increase prices at short notice. Wyndham Books reserve the right to show new retail prices on covers which may differ from those advertised in the text or elsewhere.

Postage and Packing Rate

UK: 40p for the first book, 18p for the second book and 13p for each additional book ordered to a maximum charge of £1.49p.
BFPO and EIRE: 40p for the first book, 18p for the second book, 13p per copy for the next 7 books, thereafter 7p per book.
Overseas: 60p for the first book and 18p per copy for each additional book.